CHARLES BURNS

SUGAR SKULL

PANTHEON BOOKS
NEW YORK

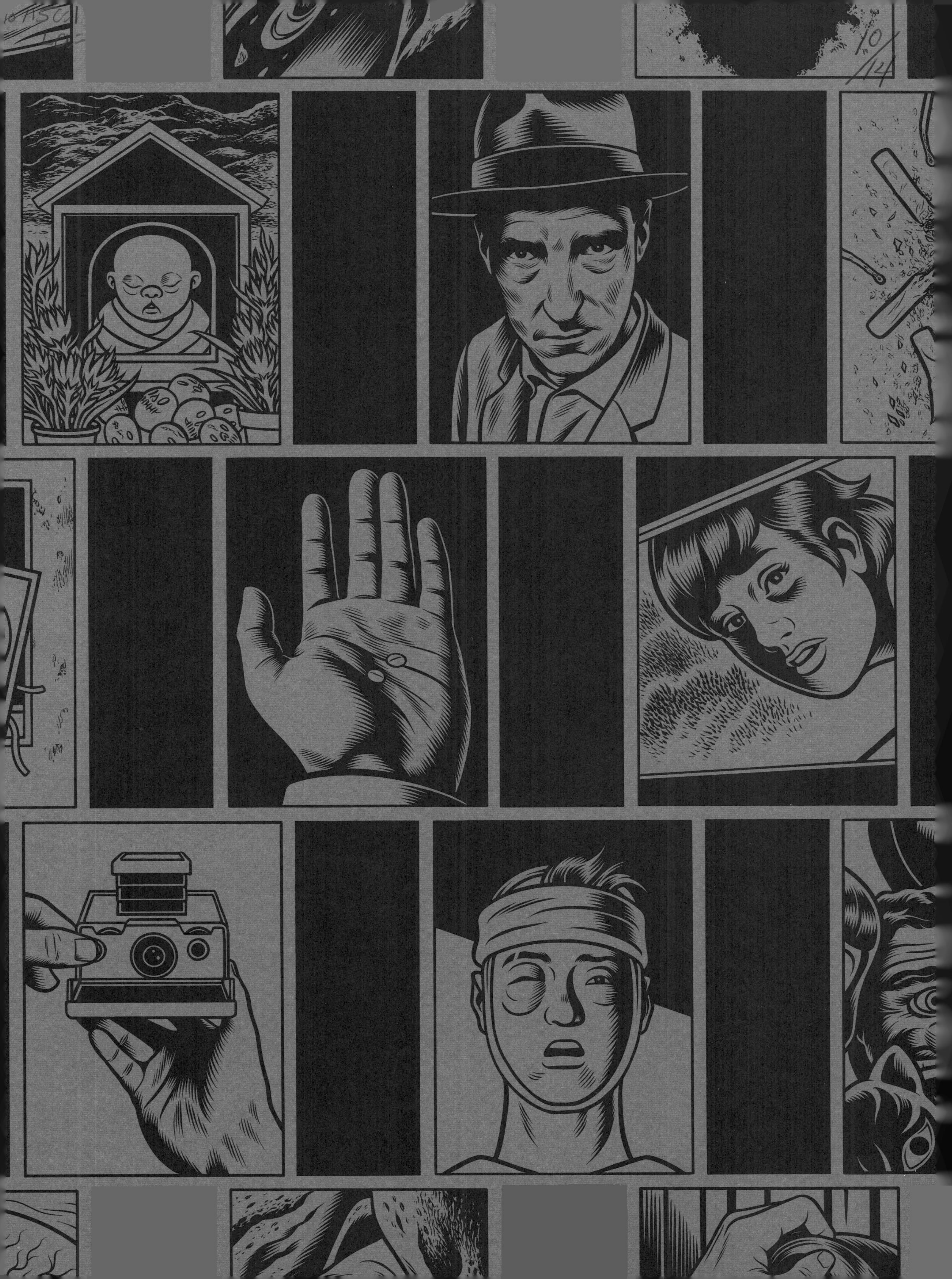

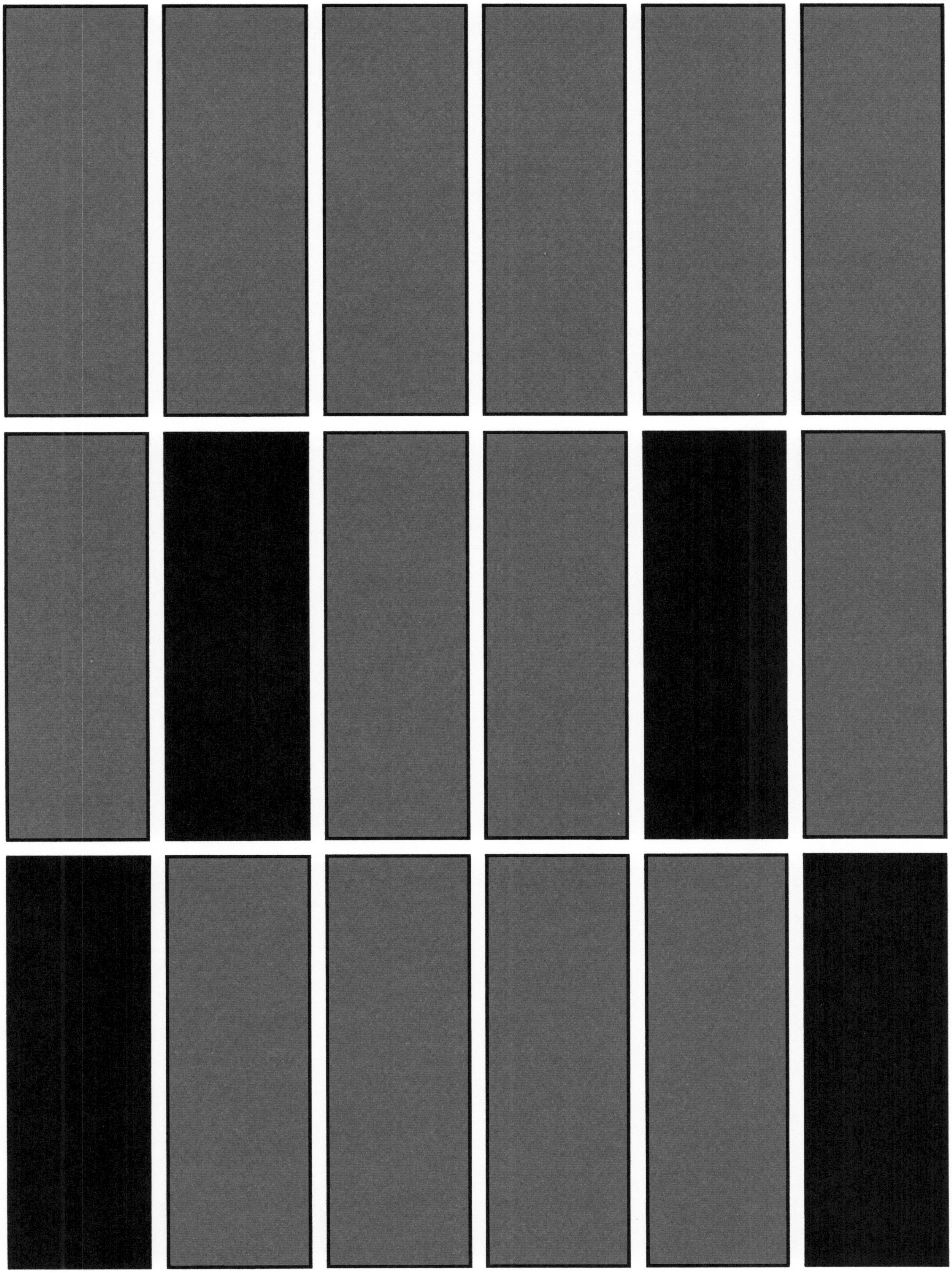

COPYRIGHT© 2014 BY CHARLES BURNS

ALL RIGHTS RESERVED. PUBLISHED
IN THE UNITED STATES BY PANTHEON
BOOKS, A DIVISION OF RANDOM
HOUSE, LLC, NEW YORK, AND IN
CANADA BY RANDOM HOUSE OF
CANADA LIMITED, TORONTO,
PENGUIN RANDOM HOUSE COMPANIES.

PANTHEON BOOKS AND COLOPHON
ARE REGISTERED TRADEMARKS OF
RANDOM HOUSE LLC.

LIBRARY OF CONGRESS CATALOGING-
IN-PUBLICATION DATA

BURNS, CHARLES.
SUGAR SKULL / CHARLES BURNS.
P. CM.
ISBN 978-0-307-90790-5
I. GRAPHIC NOVELS. I. TITLE.
PN6727.B87S94 2014
741.5'973--DC23   2014000699

WWW. PANTHEONBOOKS.COM

PRINTED IN CHINA

FIRST EDITION

9 8 7 6 5 4 3 2 1

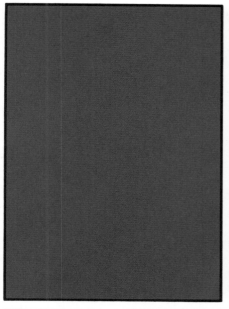

A TRAFFIC SIGNAL...

LIGHTS GO FROM GREEN TO RED.

RED ALWAYS MEANS STOP.

...BUT THAT'S NOT IT AT ALL.

IT'S A WINDOW LIT FROM WITHIN.

...AND I KNOW BETTER...

...I KNOW I SHOULDN'T LOOK.

BUT I CAN'T HELP MYSELF.

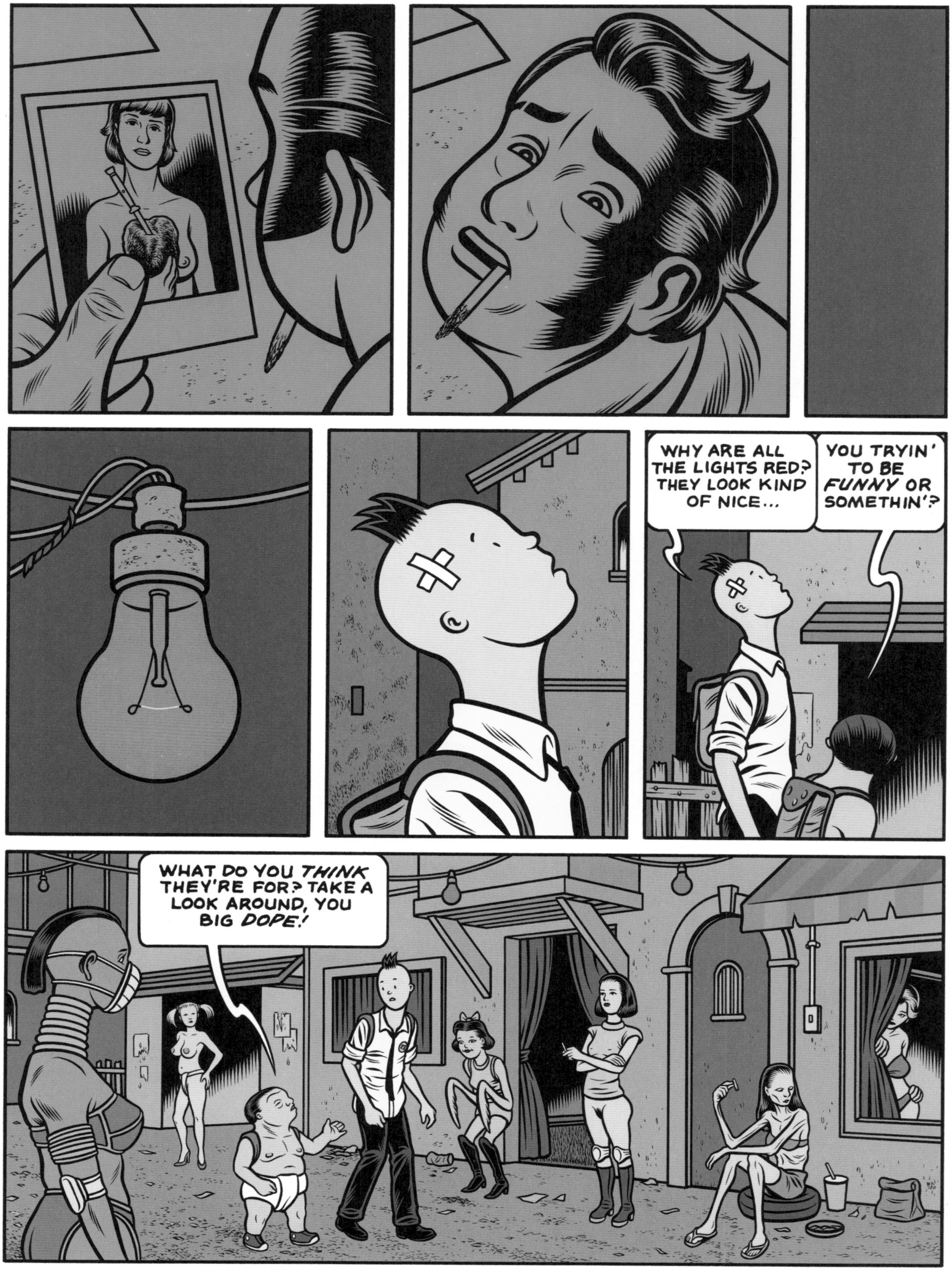
WHY ARE ALL THE LIGHTS RED? THEY LOOK KIND OF NICE...
YOU TRYIN' TO BE *FUNNY* OR SOMETHIN'?
WHAT DO YOU *THINK* THEY'RE FOR? TAKE A LOOK AROUND, YOU BIG *DOPE*!

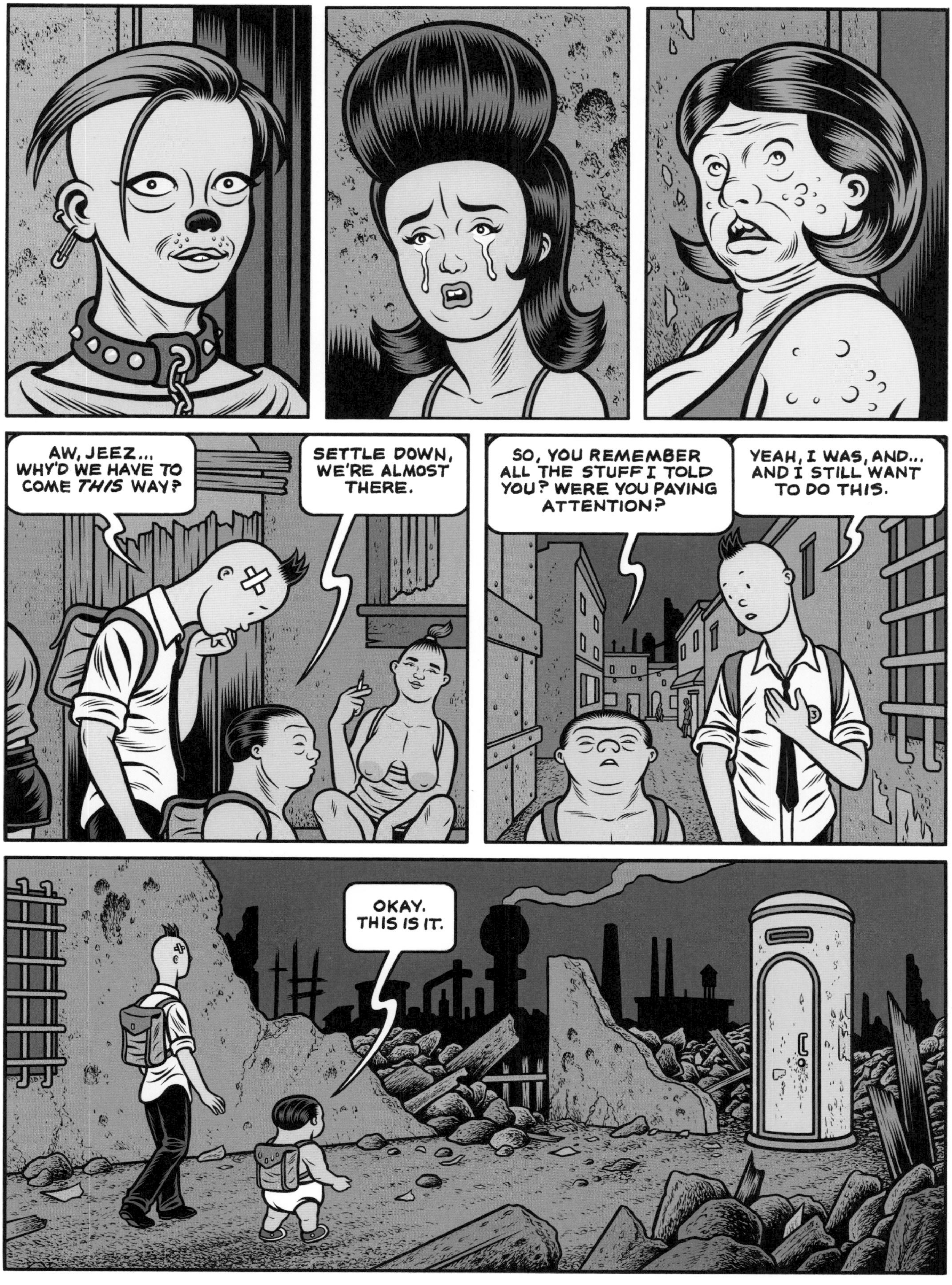
AW, JEEZ... WHY'D WE HAVE TO COME *THIS* WAY?
SETTLE DOWN, WE'RE ALMOST THERE.
SO, YOU REMEMBER ALL THE STUFF I TOLD YOU? WERE YOU PAYING ATTENTION?
YEAH, I WAS, AND... AND I STILL WANT TO DO THIS.
OKAY. THIS IS IT.

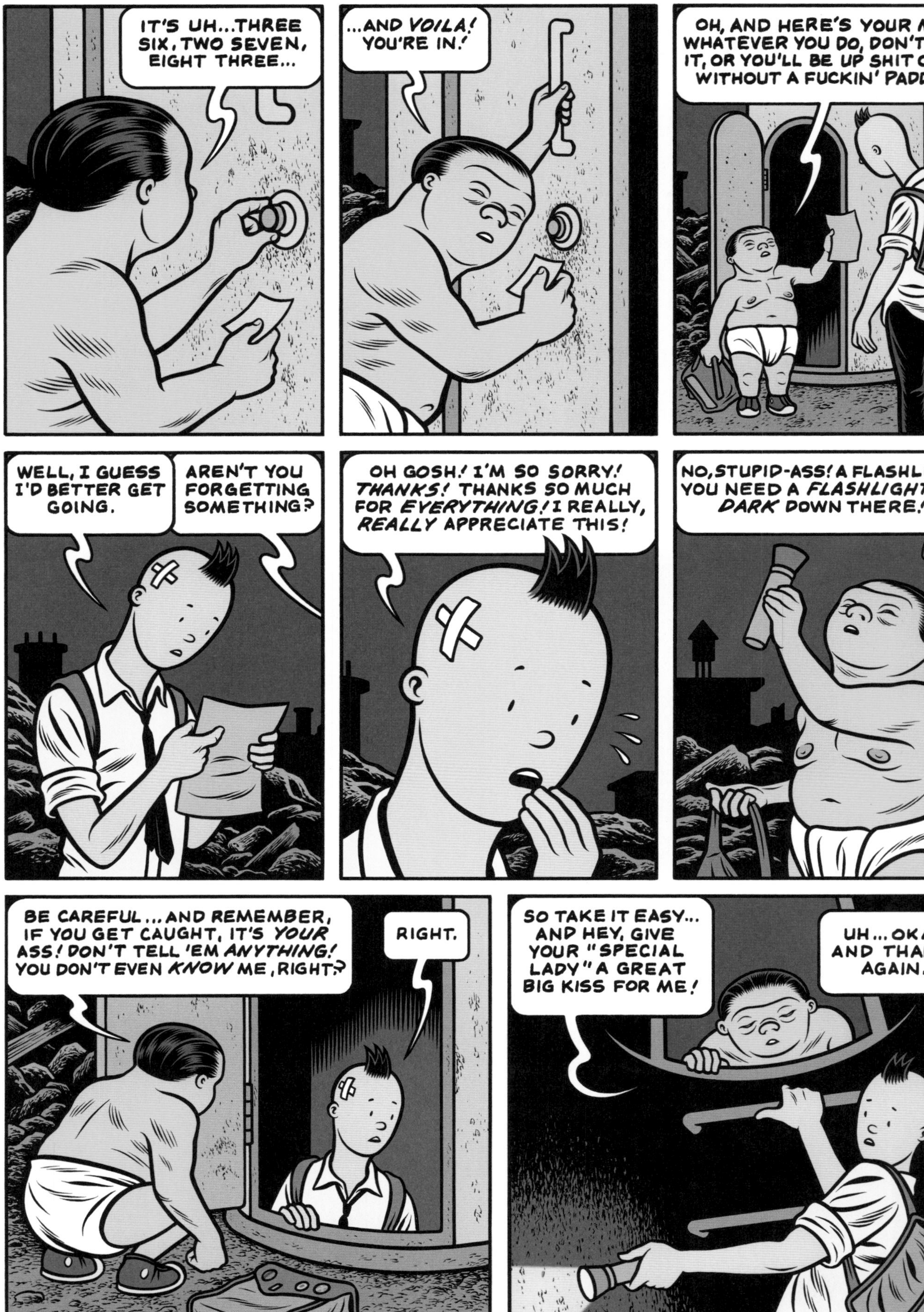
IT'S UH...THREE SIX, TWO SEVEN, EIGHT THREE...
...AND VOILA! YOU'RE IN!
OH, AND HERE'S YOUR MAP. WHATEVER YOU DO, DON'T LOSE IT, OR YOU'LL BE UP SHIT CREEK WITHOUT A FUCKIN' PADDLE!
WELL, I GUESS I'D BETTER GET GOING.
AREN'T YOU FORGETTING SOMETHING?
OH GOSH! I'M SO SORRY! THANKS! THANKS SO MUCH FOR EVERYTHING! I REALLY, REALLY APPRECIATE THIS!
NO, STUPID-ASS! A FLASHLIGHT! YOU NEED A FLASHLIGHT! IT'S DARK DOWN THERE!
BE CAREFUL... AND REMEMBER, IF YOU GET CAUGHT, IT'S YOUR ASS! DON'T TELL 'EM ANYTHING! YOU DON'T EVEN KNOW ME, RIGHT?
RIGHT.
SO TAKE IT EASY... AND HEY, GIVE YOUR "SPECIAL LADY" A GREAT BIG KISS FOR ME!
UH... OKAY, AND THANKS AGAIN.

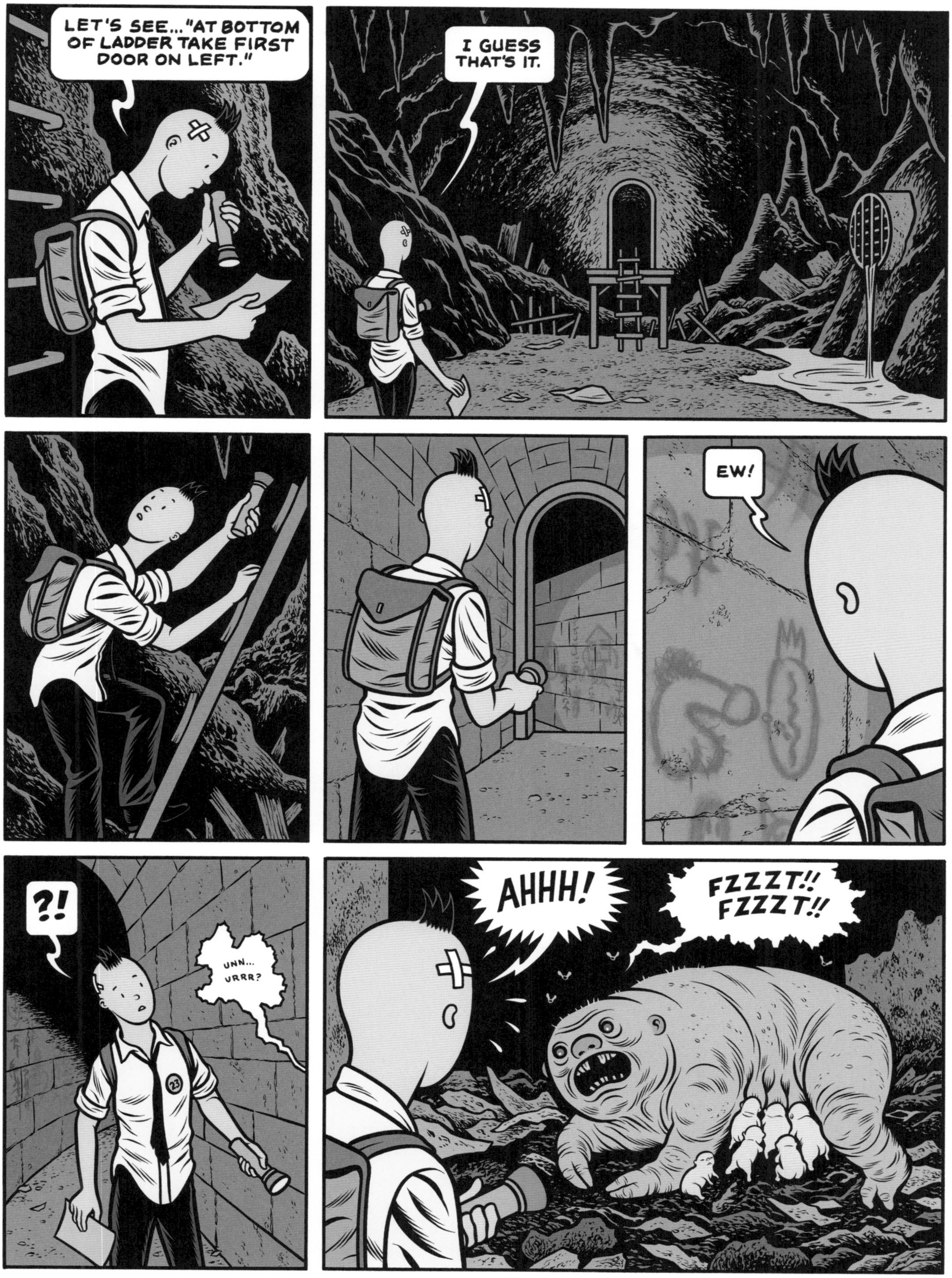
LET'S SEE..."AT BOTTOM OF LADDER TAKE FIRST DOOR ON LEFT."
I GUESS THAT'S IT.
EW!
?!
UNN... URRR?
AHHH!
FZZZT!! FZZZT!!

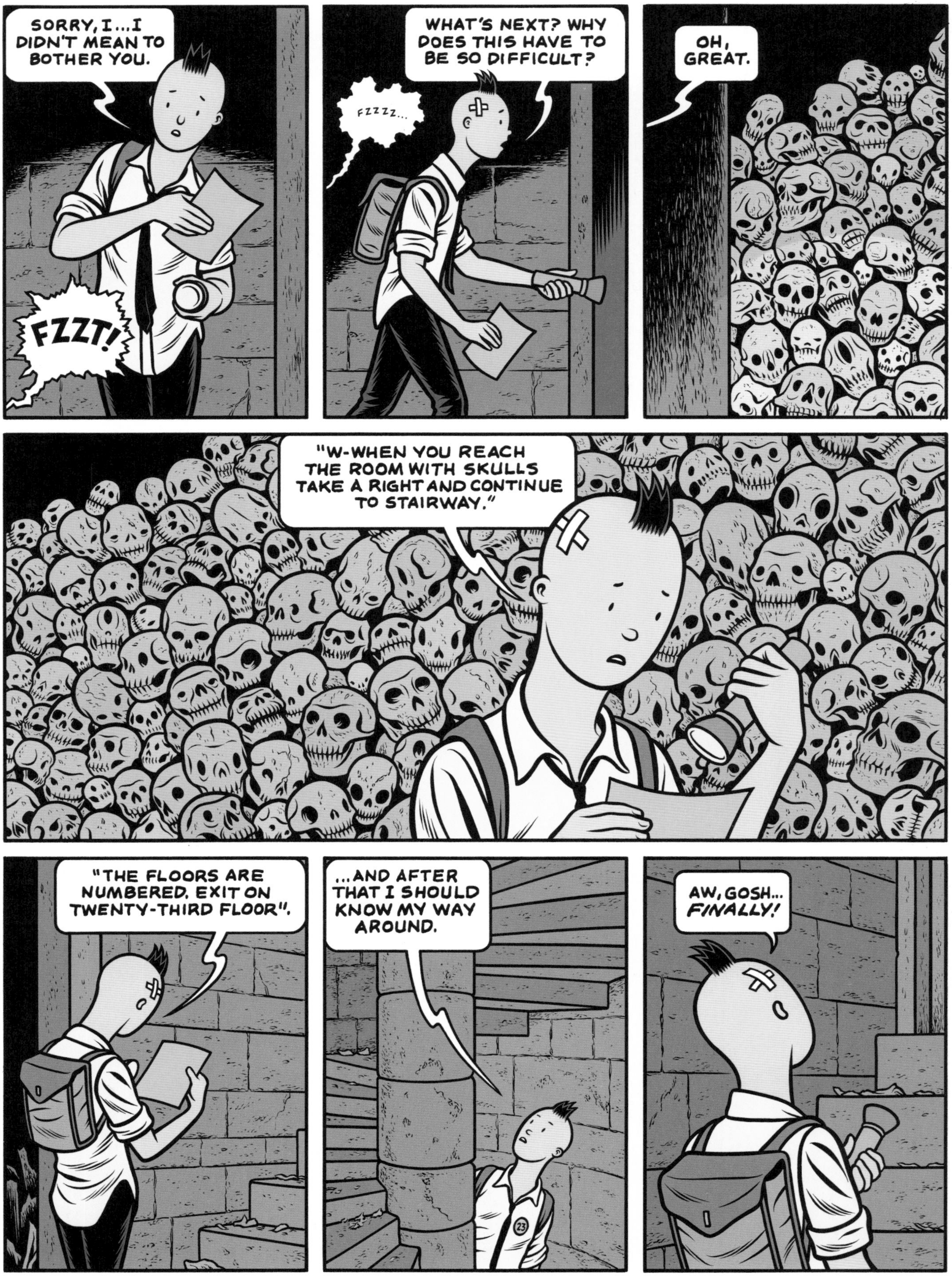
SORRY, I...I DIDN'T MEAN TO BOTHER YOU.
FZZZT!
FZZZZ...
WHAT'S NEXT? WHY DOES THIS HAVE TO BE SO DIFFICULT?
OH, GREAT.
"W-WHEN YOU REACH THE ROOM WITH SKULLS TAKE A RIGHT AND CONTINUE TO STAIRWAY."
"THE FLOORS ARE NUMBERED. EXIT ON TWENTY-THIRD FLOOR".
...AND AFTER THAT I SHOULD KNOW MY WAY AROUND.
23
AW, GOSH... *FINALLY!*

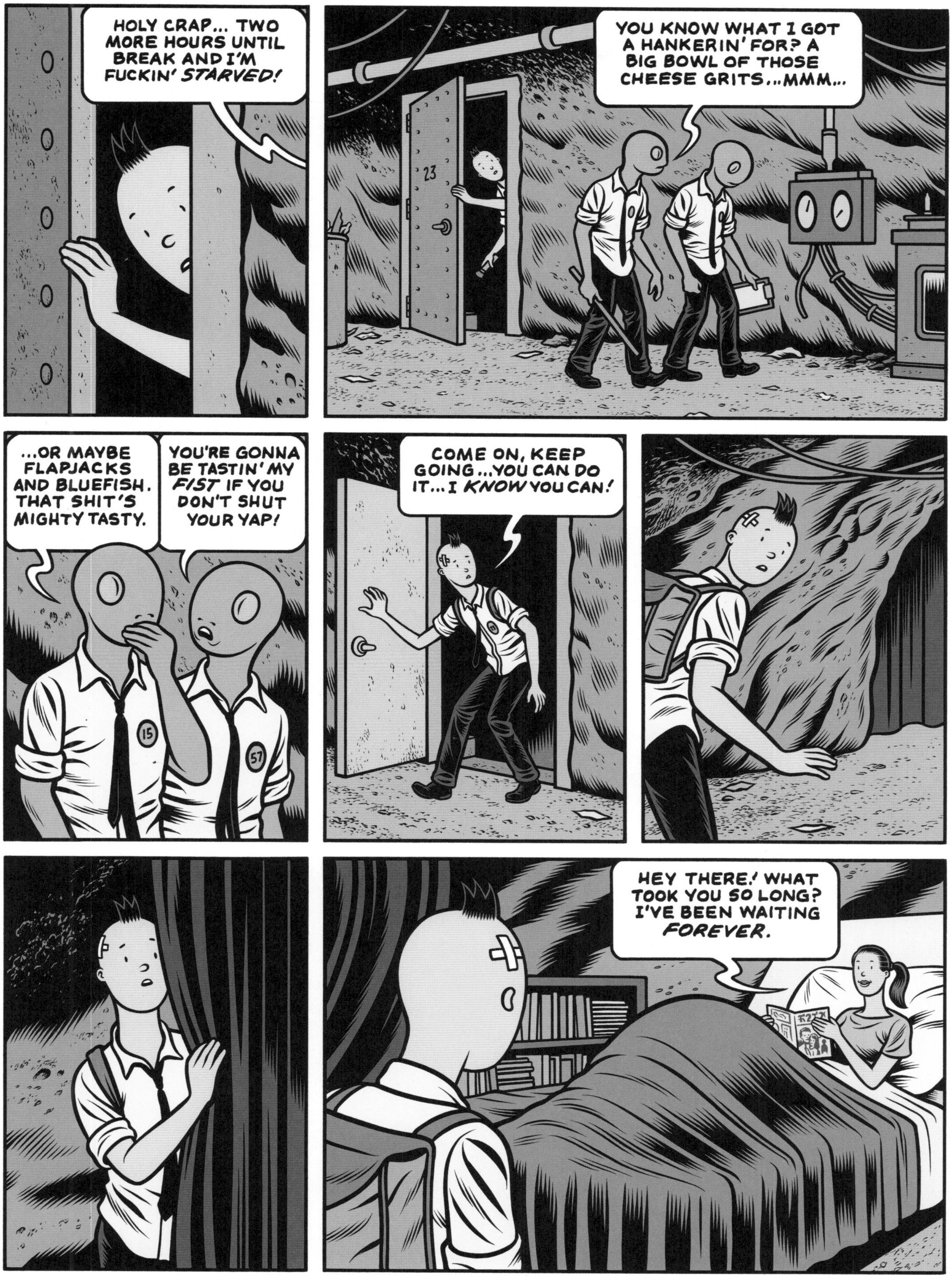
HOLY CRAP... TWO MORE HOURS UNTIL BREAK AND I'M FUCKIN' STARVED!
YOU KNOW WHAT I GOT A HANKERIN' FOR? A BIG BOWL OF THOSE CHEESE GRITS...MMM...
23
...OR MAYBE FLAPJACKS AND BLUEFISH. THAT SHIT'S MIGHTY TASTY.
YOU'RE GONNA BE TASTIN' MY FIST IF YOU DON'T SHUT YOUR YAP!
15
57
COME ON, KEEP GOING...YOU CAN DO IT...I KNOW YOU CAN!
HEY THERE! WHAT TOOK YOU SO LONG? I'VE BEEN WAITING FOREVER.

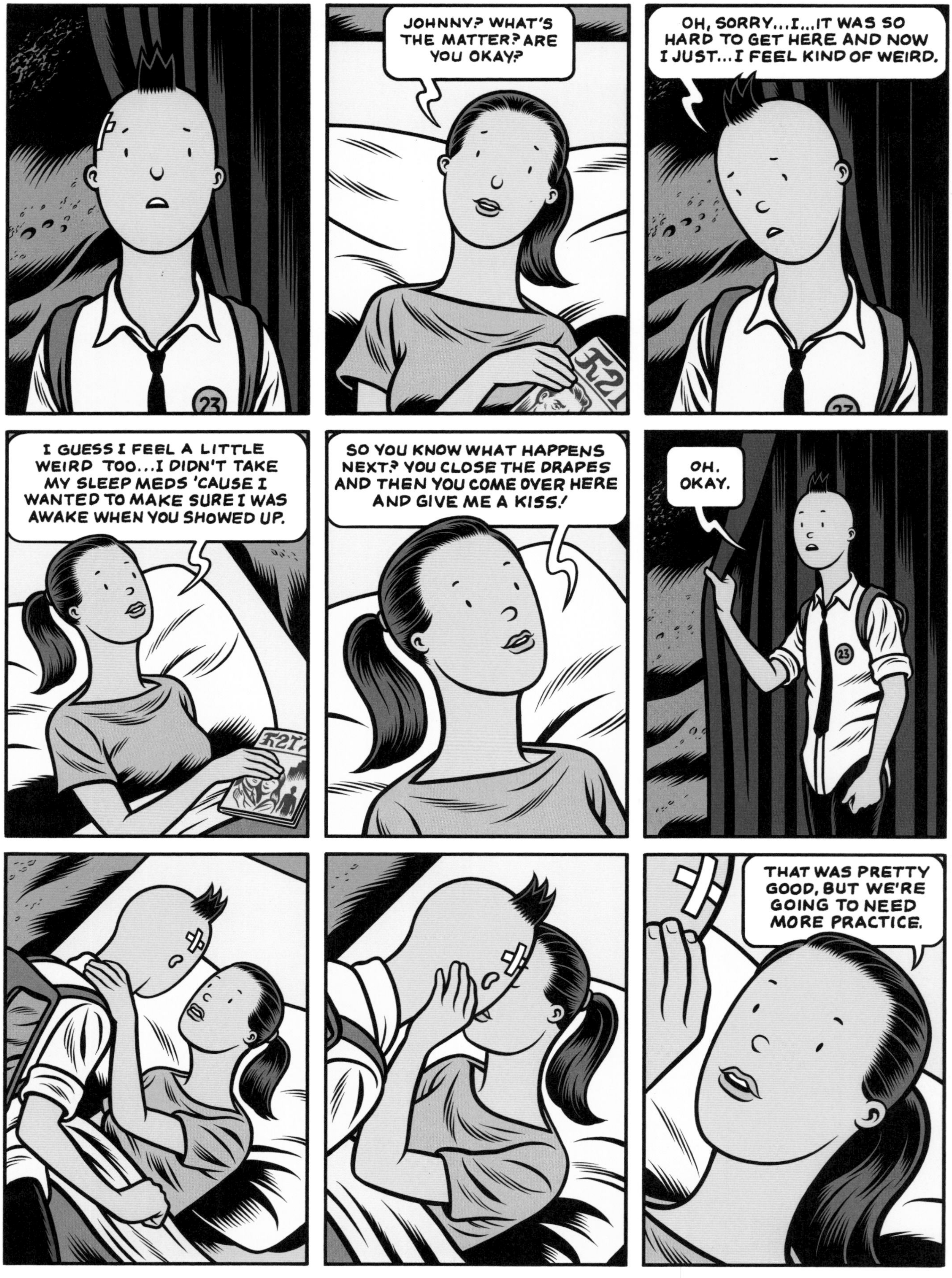
JOHNNY? WHAT'S THE MATTER? ARE YOU OKAY?
OH, SORRY...I...IT WAS SO HARD TO GET HERE AND NOW I JUST...I FEEL KIND OF WEIRD.
I GUESS I FEEL A LITTLE WEIRD TOO...I DIDN'T TAKE MY SLEEP MEDS 'CAUSE I WANTED TO MAKE SURE I WAS AWAKE WHEN YOU SHOWED UP.
SO YOU KNOW WHAT HAPPENS NEXT? YOU CLOSE THE DRAPES AND THEN YOU COME OVER HERE AND GIVE ME A KISS!
OH. OKAY.
THAT WAS PRETTY GOOD, BUT WE'RE GOING TO NEED MORE PRACTICE.

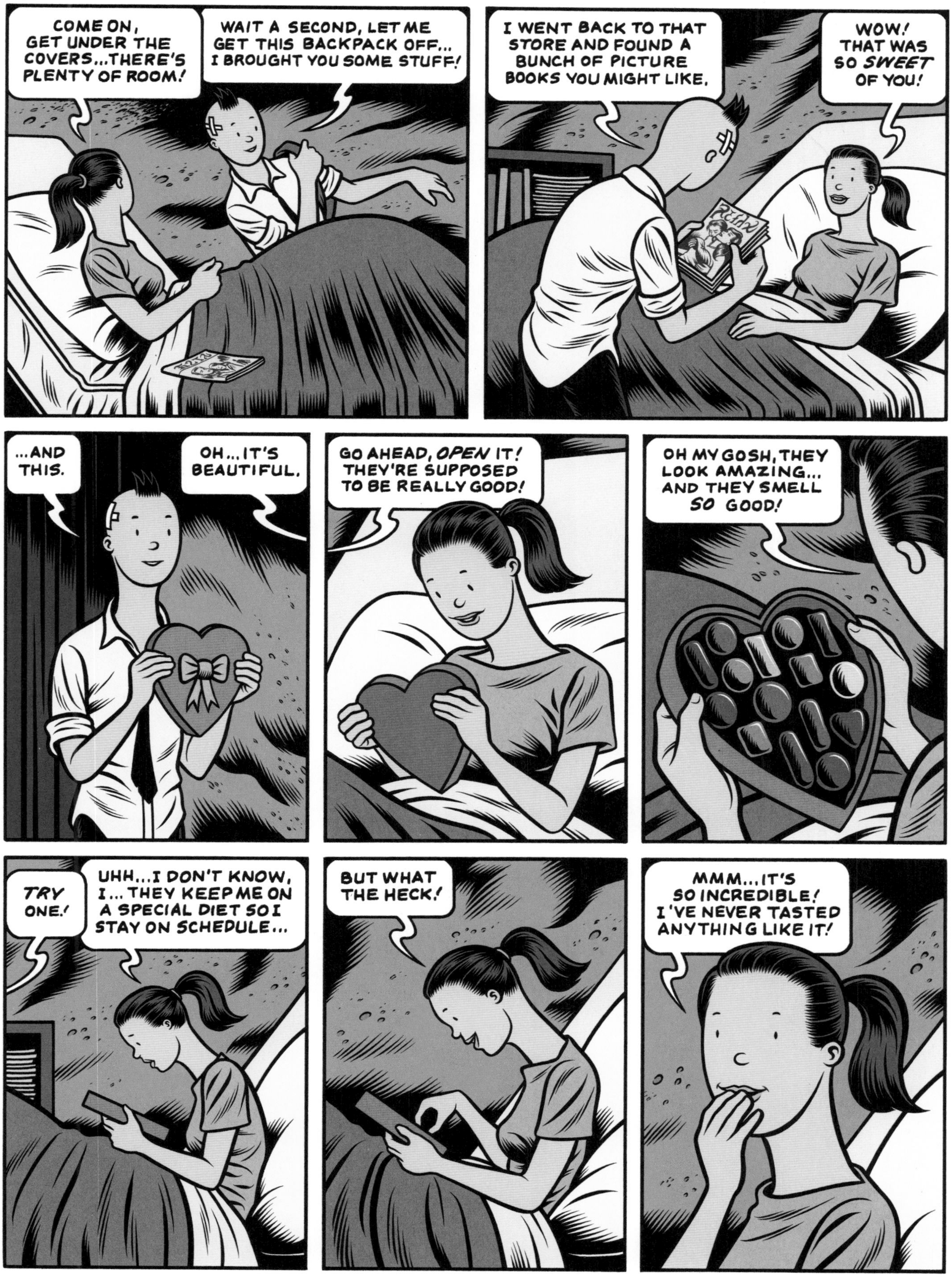
COME ON, GET UNDER THE COVERS...THERE'S PLENTY OF ROOM!
WAIT A SECOND, LET ME GET THIS BACKPACK OFF... I BROUGHT YOU SOME STUFF!
I WENT BACK TO THAT STORE AND FOUND A BUNCH OF PICTURE BOOKS YOU MIGHT LIKE.
WOW! THAT WAS SO *SWEET* OF YOU!
...AND THIS.
OH... IT'S BEAUTIFUL.
GO AHEAD, *OPEN* IT! THEY'RE SUPPOSED TO BE REALLY GOOD!
OH MY GOSH, THEY LOOK AMAZING... AND THEY SMELL *SO* GOOD!
TRY ONE!
UHH...I DON'T KNOW, I... THEY KEEP ME ON A SPECIAL DIET SO I STAY ON SCHEDULE...
BUT WHAT THE HECK!
MMM...IT'S SO INCREDIBLE! I'VE NEVER TASTED ANYTHING LIKE IT!

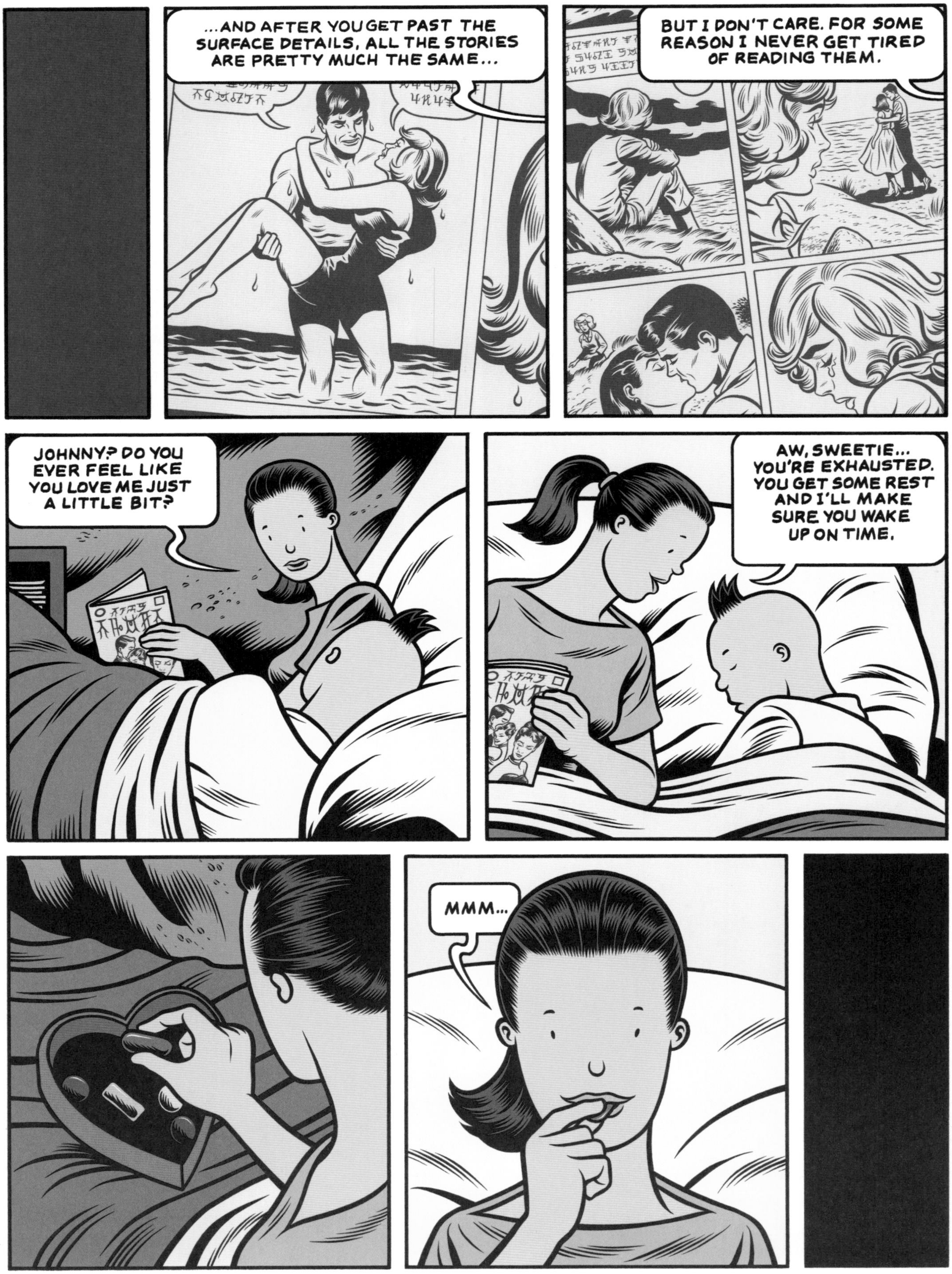
...AND AFTER YOU GET PAST THE SURFACE DETAILS, ALL THE STORIES ARE PRETTY MUCH THE SAME...
BUT I DON'T CARE. FOR SOME REASON I NEVER GET TIRED OF READING THEM.
JOHNNY? DO YOU EVER FEEL LIKE YOU LOVE ME JUST A LITTLE BIT?
AW, SWEETIE... YOU'RE EXHAUSTED. YOU GET SOME REST AND I'LL MAKE SURE YOU WAKE UP ON TIME.
MMM...

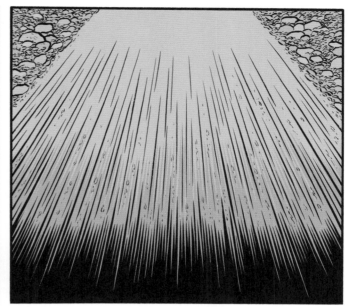

COME ON, SPORT... YOU'VE GOT A JOB TO DO.

I'M NEVER SURPRISED WHEN HE SHOWS UP.

ONE WAY OR THE OTHER, HE'S ALWAYS THERE.

BUT WHY ME? WHY DO I HAVE TO BE THE ONE?

BECAUSE I SAID SO. AND BECAUSE YOU PROMISED.

THAT VOICE.

NO MATTER WHAT I DO I'LL NEVER GET RID OF THAT VOICE IN MY HEAD.

COME ON, IT'S NOTHING...JUST A FEW OLD ASHES.

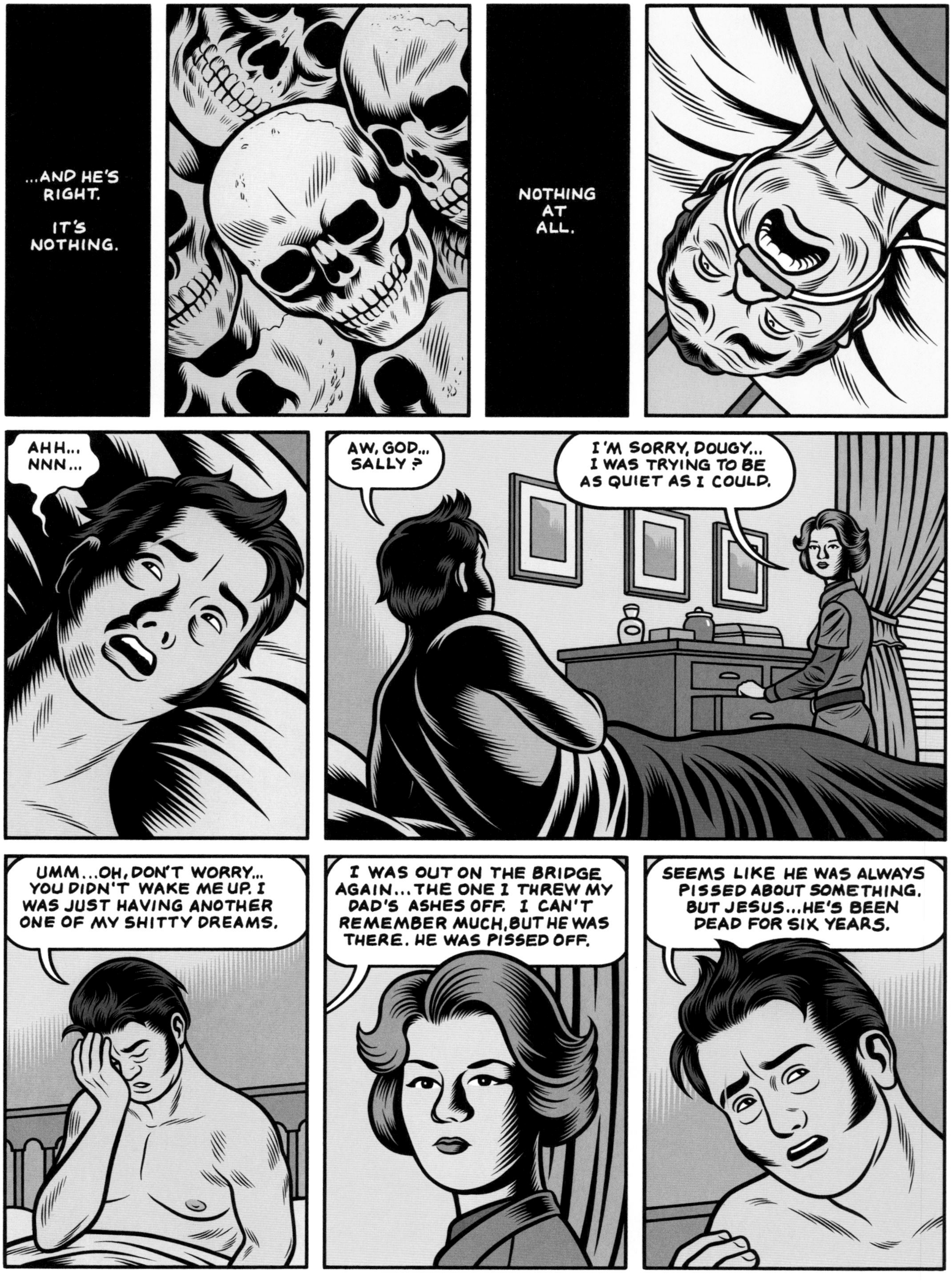
...AND HE'S RIGHT.
IT'S NOTHING.
NOTHING AT ALL.
AHH... NNN...
AW, GOD... SALLY ?
I'M SORRY, DOUGY... I WAS TRYING TO BE AS QUIET AS I COULD.
UMM...OH, DON'T WORRY... YOU DIDN'T WAKE ME UP. I WAS JUST HAVING ANOTHER ONE OF MY SHITTY DREAMS.
I WAS OUT ON THE BRIDGE AGAIN... THE ONE I THREW MY DAD'S ASHES OFF. I CAN'T REMEMBER MUCH, BUT HE WAS THERE. HE WAS PISSED OFF.
SEEMS LIKE HE WAS ALWAYS PISSED ABOUT SOMETHING. BUT JESUS...HE'S BEEN DEAD FOR SIX YEARS.

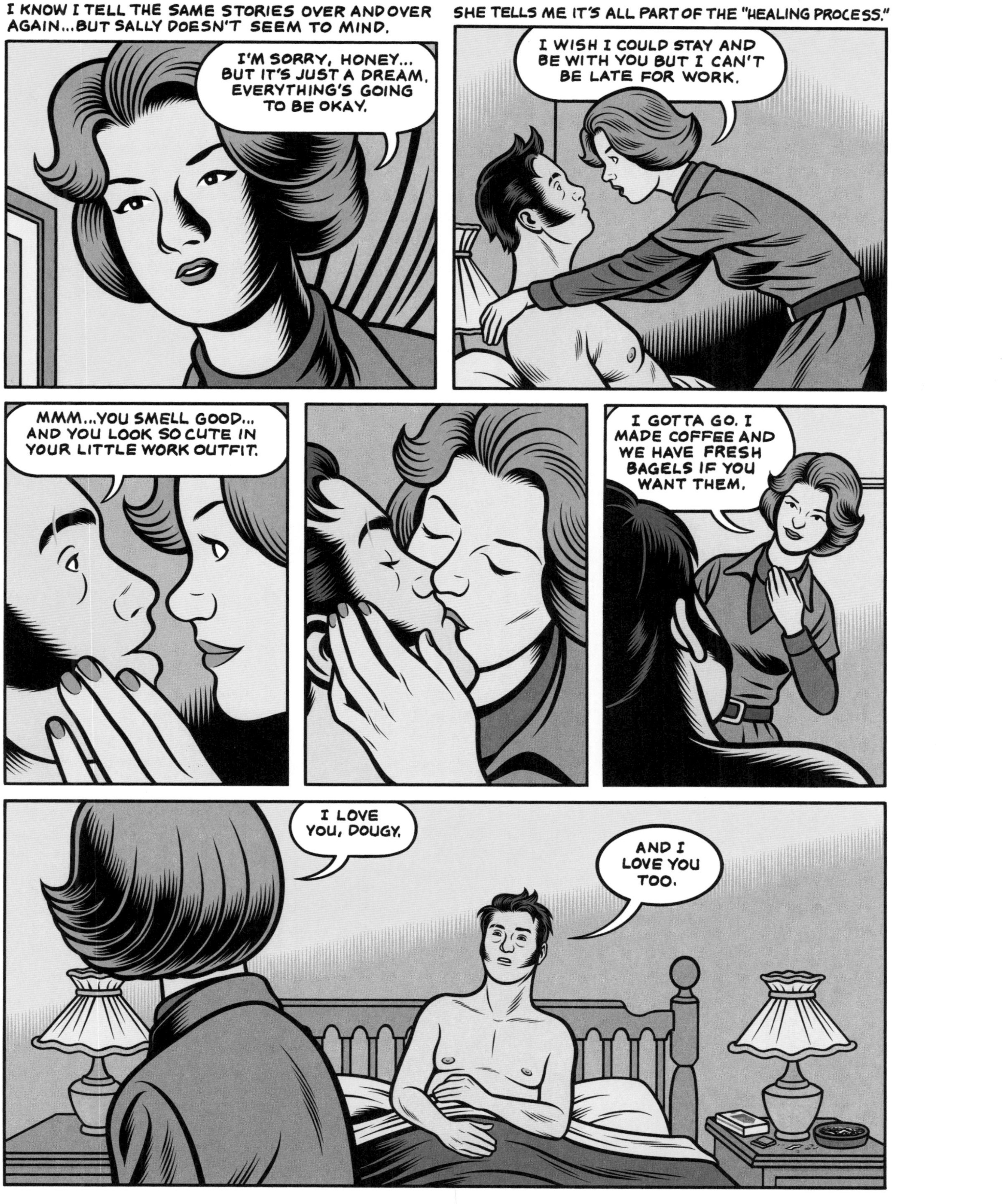
I KNOW I TELL THE SAME STORIES OVER AND OVER AGAIN... BUT SALLY DOESN'T SEEM TO MIND.
I'M SORRY, HONEY... BUT IT'S JUST A DREAM. EVERYTHING'S GOING TO BE OKAY.
SHE TELLS ME IT'S ALL PART OF THE "HEALING PROCESS."
I WISH I COULD STAY AND BE WITH YOU BUT I CAN'T BE LATE FOR WORK.
MMM... YOU SMELL GOOD... AND YOU LOOK SO CUTE IN YOUR LITTLE WORK OUTFIT.
I GOTTA GO. I MADE COFFEE AND WE HAVE FRESH BAGELS IF YOU WANT THEM.
I LOVE YOU, DOUGY.
AND I LOVE YOU TOO.

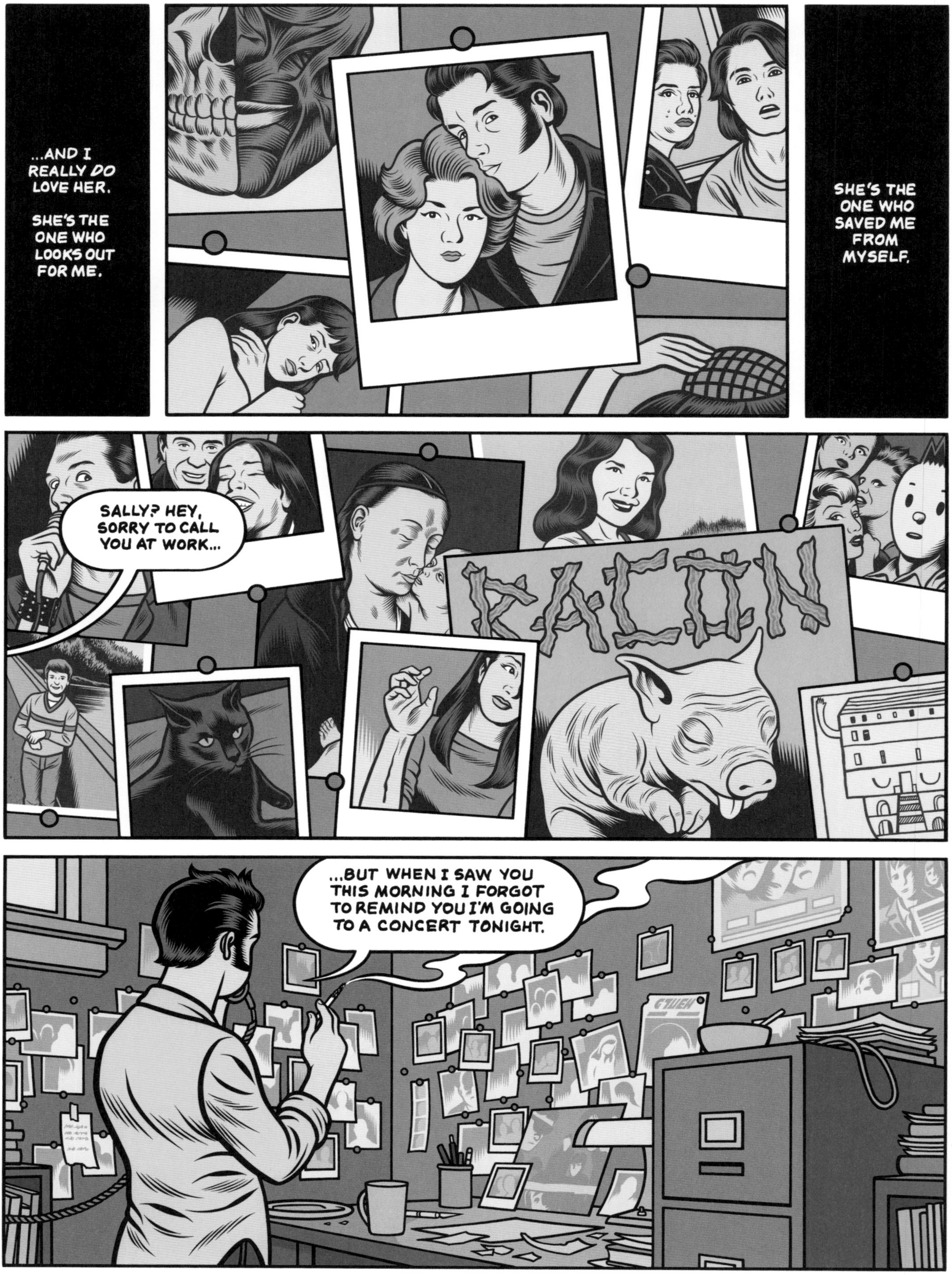
...AND I REALLY *DO* LOVE HER.
SHE'S THE ONE WHO LOOKS OUT FOR ME.
SHE'S THE ONE WHO SAVED ME FROM MYSELF.
SALLY? HEY, SORRY TO CALL YOU AT WORK...
...BUT WHEN I SAW YOU THIS MORNING I FORGOT TO REMIND YOU I'M GOING TO A CONCERT TONIGHT.

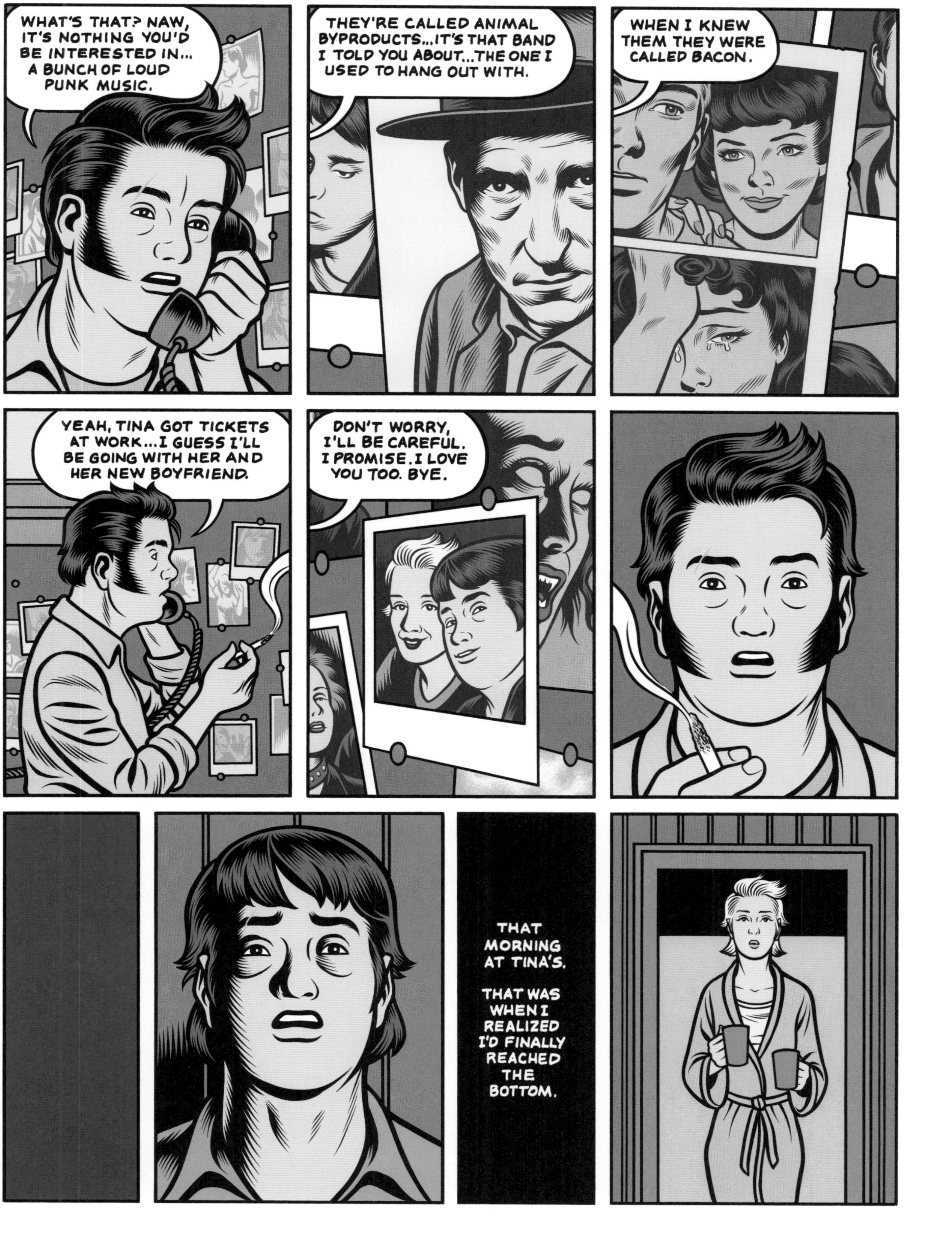
WHAT'S THAT? NAW, IT'S NOTHING YOU'D BE INTERESTED IN... A BUNCH OF LOUD PUNK MUSIC.
THEY'RE CALLED ANIMAL BYPRODUCTS...IT'S THAT BAND I TOLD YOU ABOUT...THE ONE I USED TO HANG OUT WITH.
WHEN I KNEW THEM THEY WERE CALLED BACON.
YEAH, TINA GOT TICKETS AT WORK...I GUESS I'LL BE GOING WITH HER AND HER NEW BOYFRIEND.
DON'T WORRY, I'LL BE CAREFUL. I PROMISE. I LOVE YOU TOO. BYE.
THAT MORNING AT TINA'S.
THAT WAS WHEN I REALIZED I'D FINALLY REACHED THE BOTTOM.

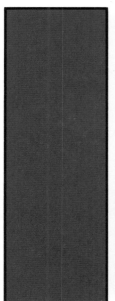

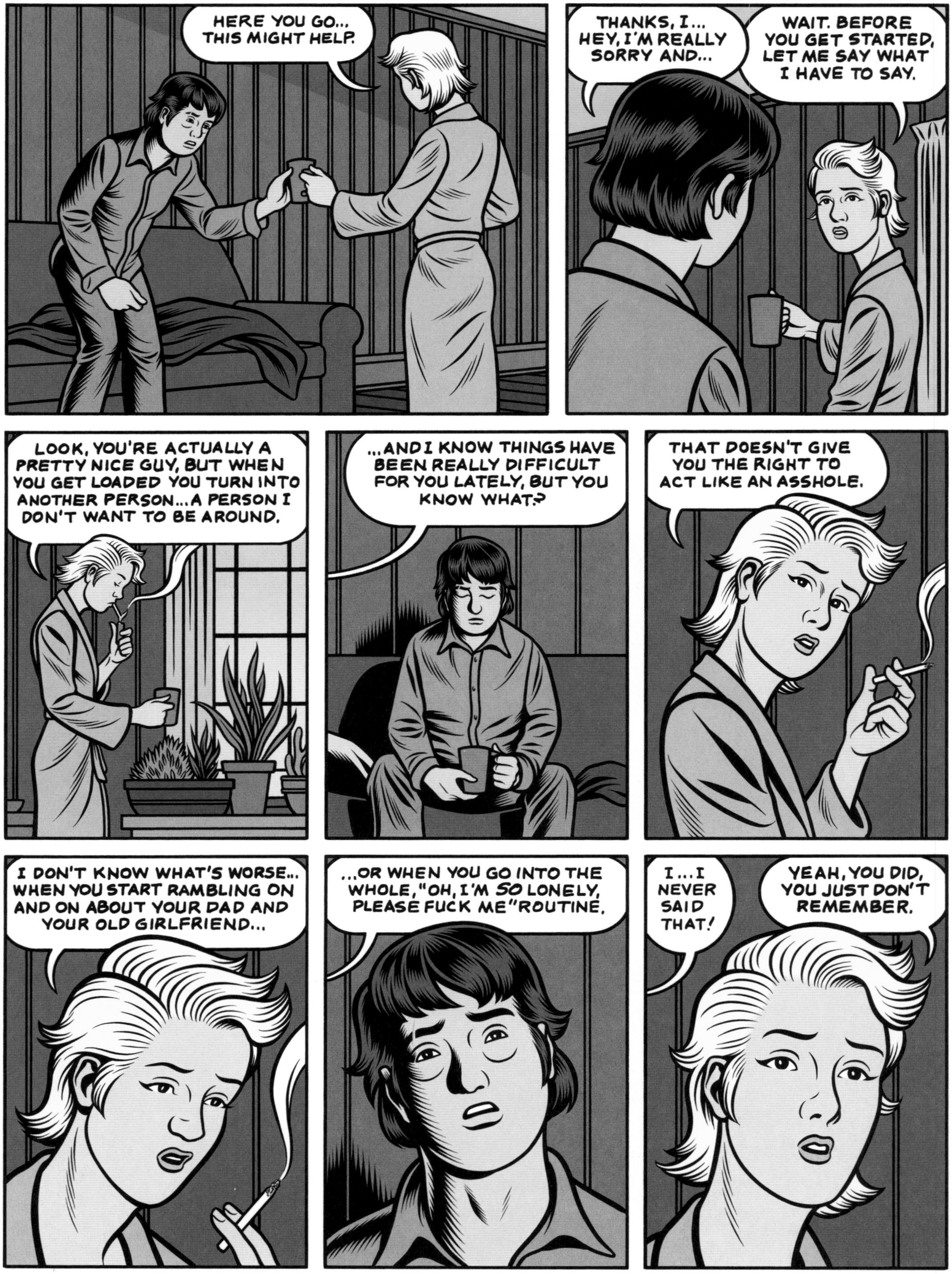

HERE YOU GO... THIS MIGHT HELP.
THANKS, I... HEY, I'M REALLY SORRY AND...
WAIT. BEFORE YOU GET STARTED, LET ME SAY WHAT I HAVE TO SAY.
LOOK, YOU'RE ACTUALLY A PRETTY NICE GUY, BUT WHEN YOU GET LOADED YOU TURN INTO ANOTHER PERSON... A PERSON I DON'T WANT TO BE AROUND.
...AND I KNOW THINGS HAVE BEEN REALLY DIFFICULT FOR YOU LATELY, BUT YOU KNOW WHAT?
THAT DOESN'T GIVE YOU THE RIGHT TO ACT LIKE AN ASSHOLE.
I DON'T KNOW WHAT'S WORSE... WHEN YOU START RAMBLING ON AND ON ABOUT YOUR DAD AND YOUR OLD GIRLFRIEND...
...OR WHEN YOU GO INTO THE WHOLE, "OH, I'M SO LONELY, PLEASE FUCK ME" ROUTINE.
I... I NEVER SAID THAT!
YEAH, YOU DID, YOU JUST DON'T REMEMBER.

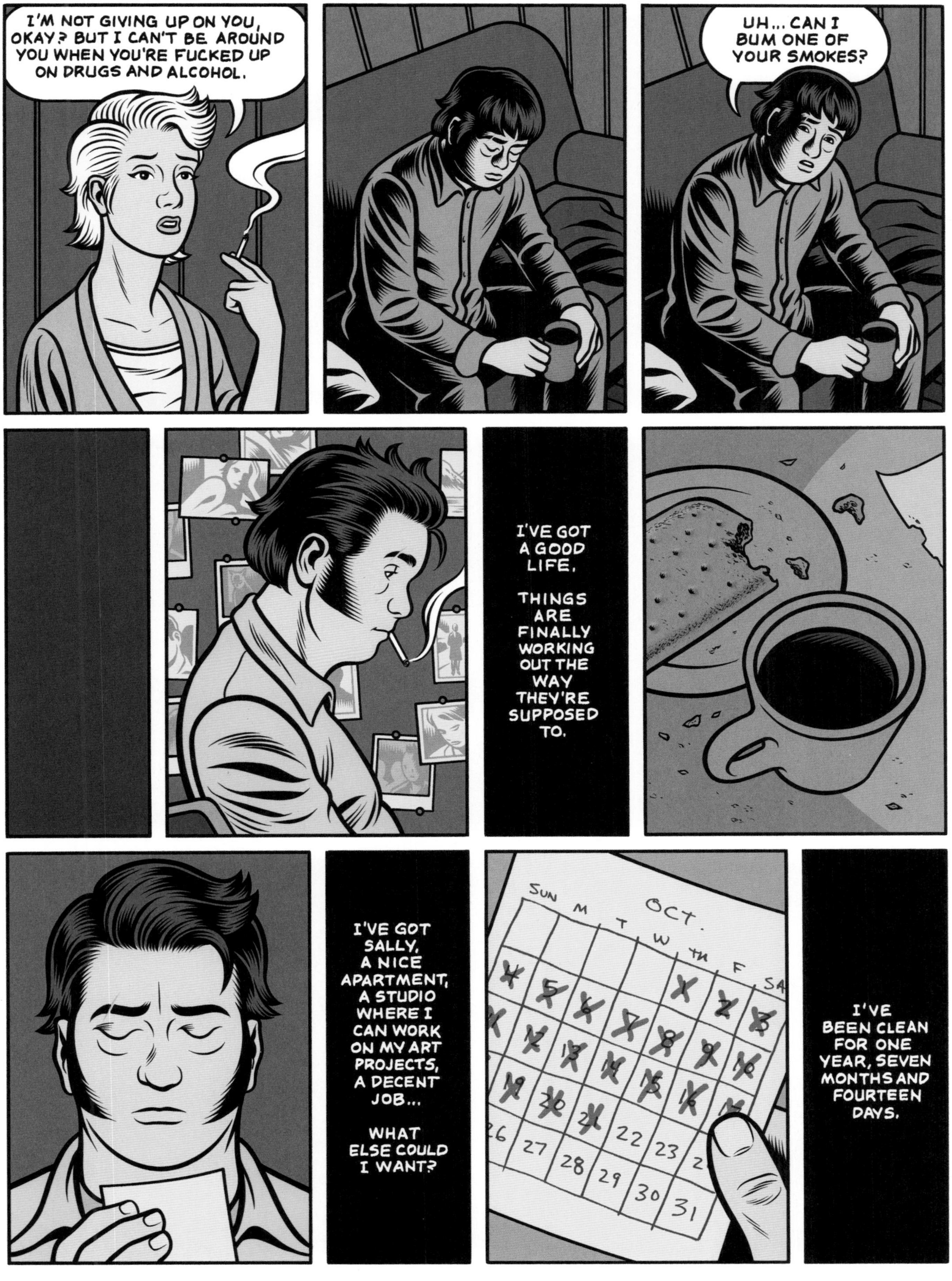

I'M NOT GIVING UP ON YOU, OKAY? BUT I CAN'T BE AROUND YOU WHEN YOU'RE FUCKED UP ON DRUGS AND ALCOHOL.
UH... CAN I BUM ONE OF YOUR SMOKES?
I'VE GOT A GOOD LIFE.
THINGS ARE FINALLY WORKING OUT THE WAY THEY'RE SUPPOSED TO.
I'VE GOT SALLY, A NICE APARTMENT, A STUDIO WHERE I CAN WORK ON MY ART PROJECTS, A DECENT JOB...
WHAT ELSE COULD I WANT?
OCT.
I'VE BEEN CLEAN FOR ONE YEAR, SEVEN MONTHS AND FOURTEEN DAYS.

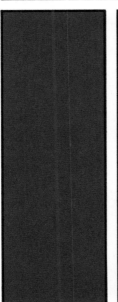

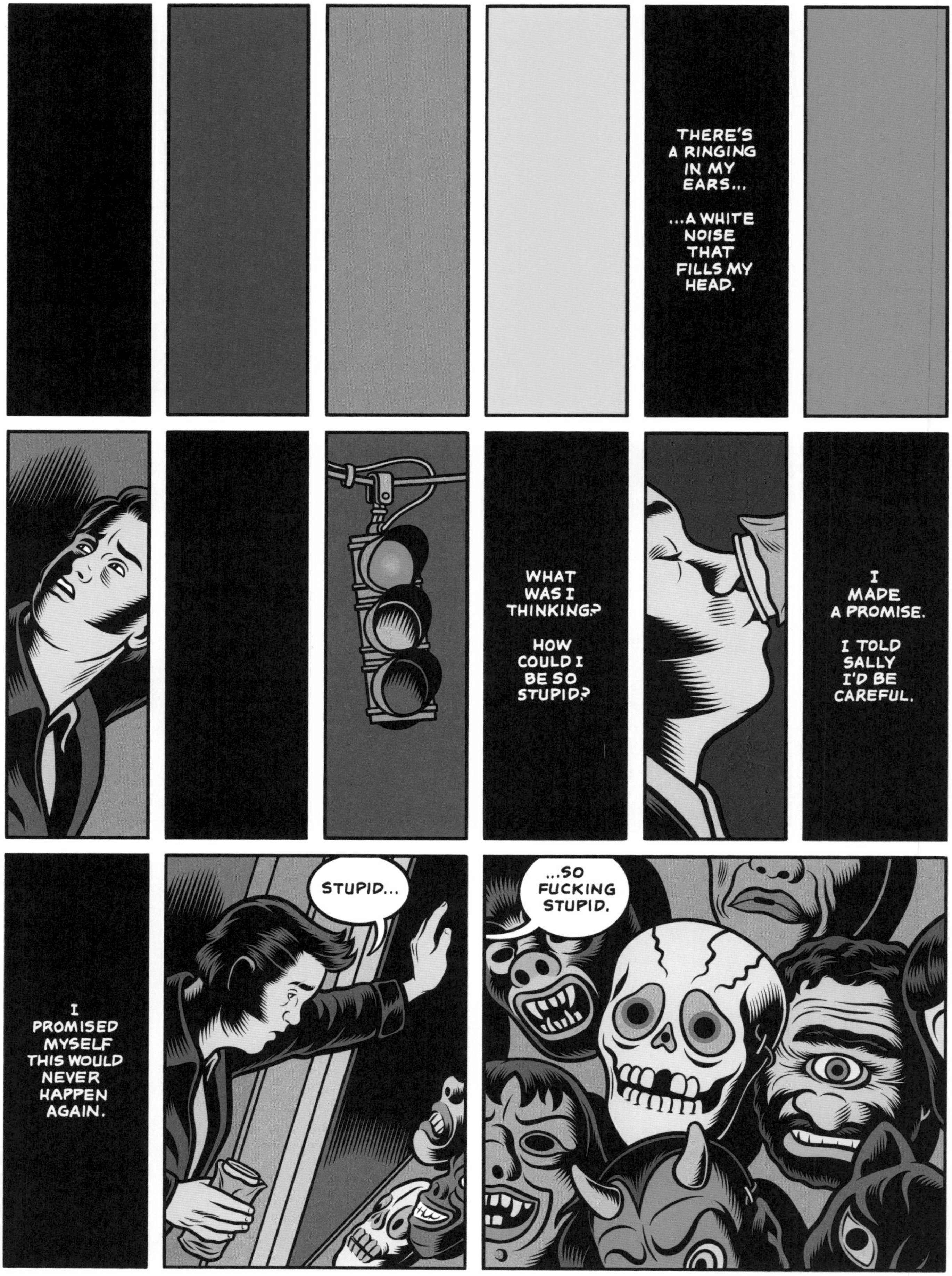
THERE'S A RINGING IN MY EARS...
...A WHITE NOISE THAT FILLS MY HEAD.
WHAT WAS I THINKING?
HOW COULD I BE SO STUPID?
I MADE A PROMISE.
I TOLD SALLY I'D BE CAREFUL.
I PROMISED MYSELF THIS WOULD NEVER HAPPEN AGAIN.
STUPID...
...SO FUCKING STUPID.

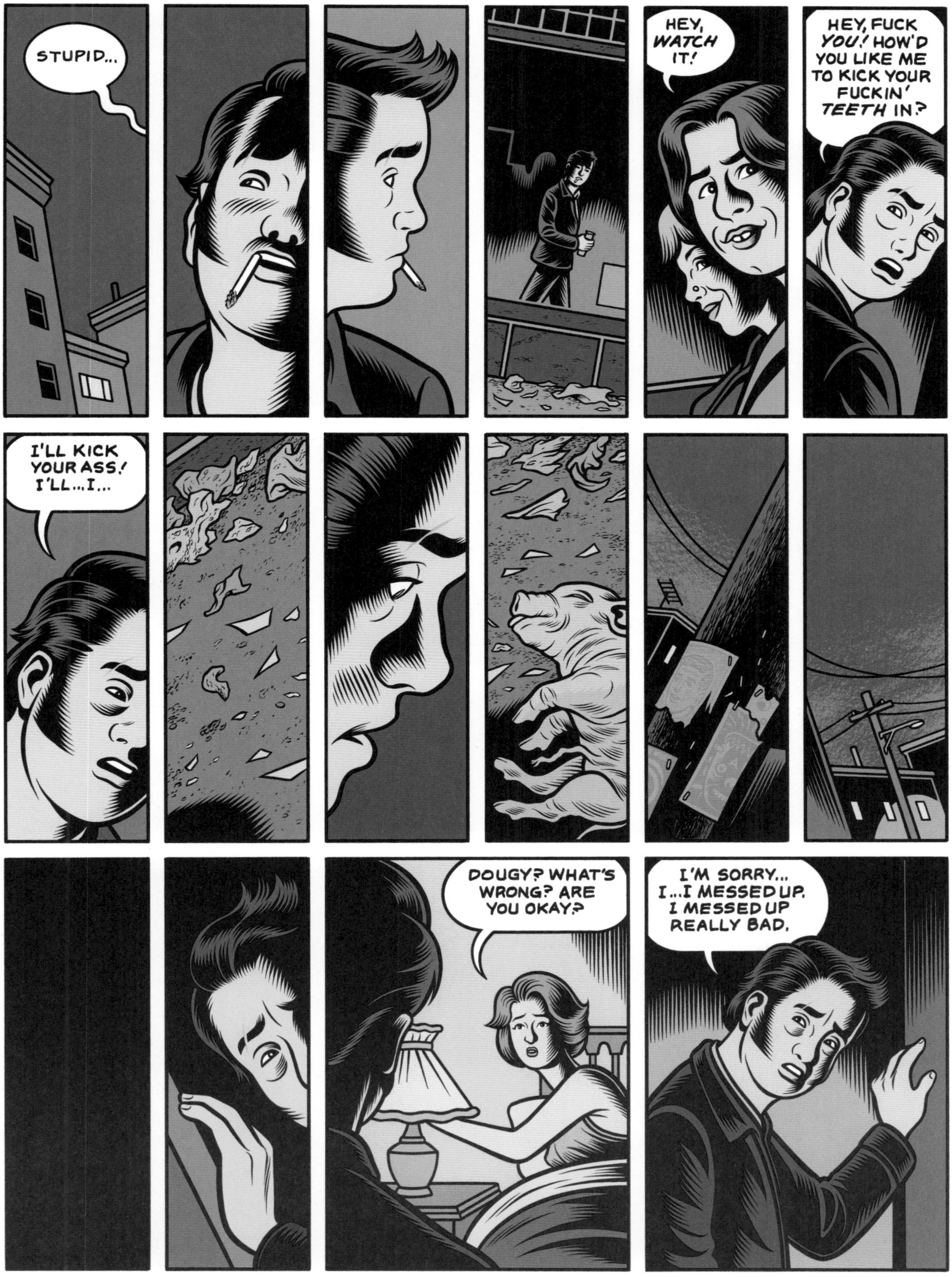
STUPID...
HEY, WATCH IT!
HEY, FUCK YOU! HOW'D YOU LIKE ME TO KICK YOUR FUCKIN' TEETH IN?
I'LL KICK YOUR ASS! I'LL...I...
DOUGY? WHAT'S WRONG? ARE YOU OKAY?
I'M SORRY... I...I MESSED UP. I MESSED UP REALLY BAD.

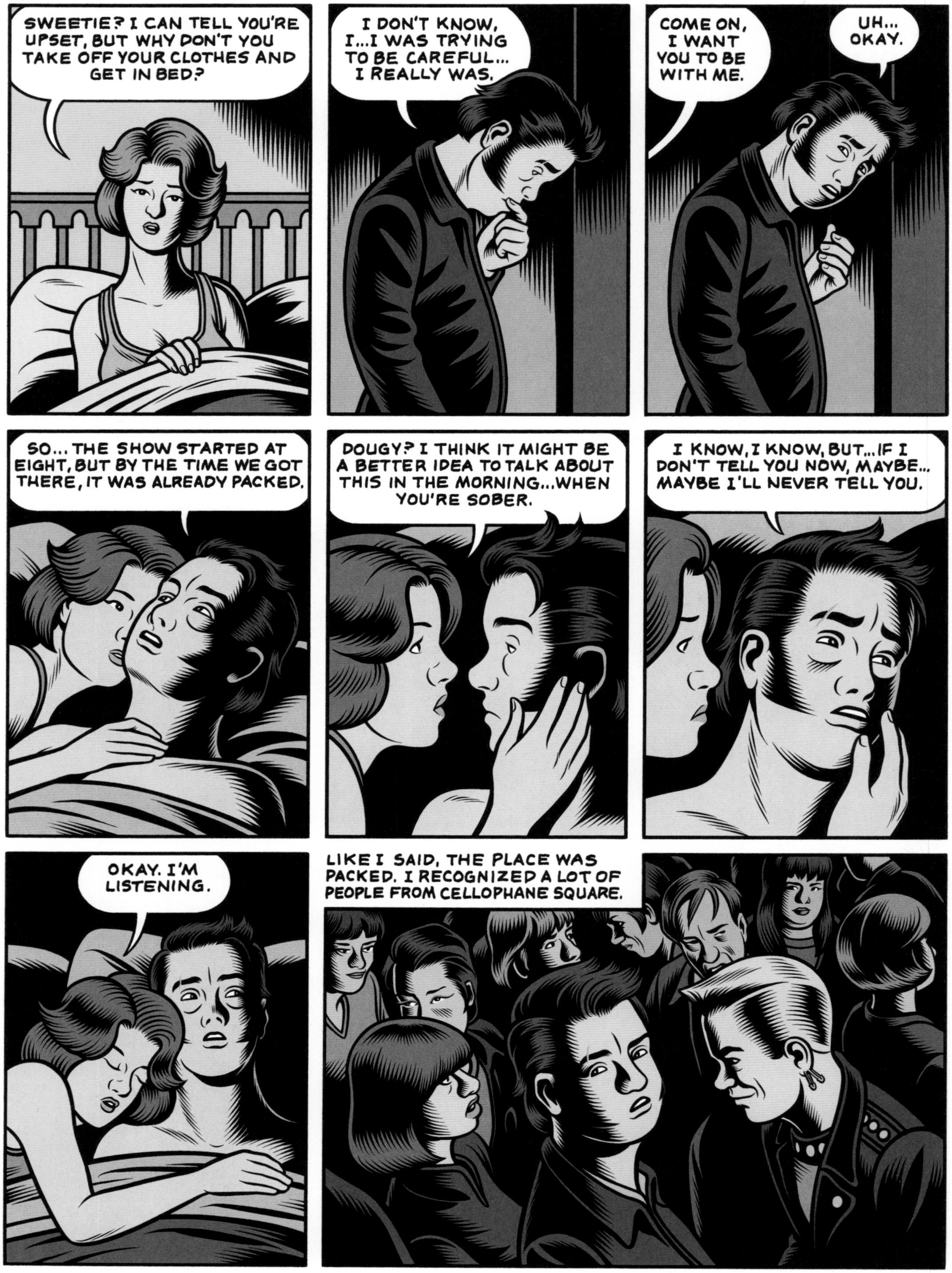
SWEETIE? I CAN TELL YOU'RE UPSET, BUT WHY DON'T YOU TAKE OFF YOUR CLOTHES AND GET IN BED?
I DON'T KNOW, I...I WAS TRYING TO BE CAREFUL... I REALLY WAS.
COME ON, I WANT YOU TO BE WITH ME.
UH... OKAY.
SO... THE SHOW STARTED AT EIGHT, BUT BY THE TIME WE GOT THERE, IT WAS ALREADY PACKED.
DOUGY? I THINK IT MIGHT BE A BETTER IDEA TO TALK ABOUT THIS IN THE MORNING...WHEN YOU'RE SOBER.
I KNOW, I KNOW, BUT...IF I DON'T TELL YOU NOW, MAYBE... MAYBE I'LL NEVER TELL YOU.
OKAY. I'M LISTENING.
LIKE I SAID, THE PLACE WAS PACKED. I RECOGNIZED A LOT OF PEOPLE FROM CELLOPHANE SQUARE.

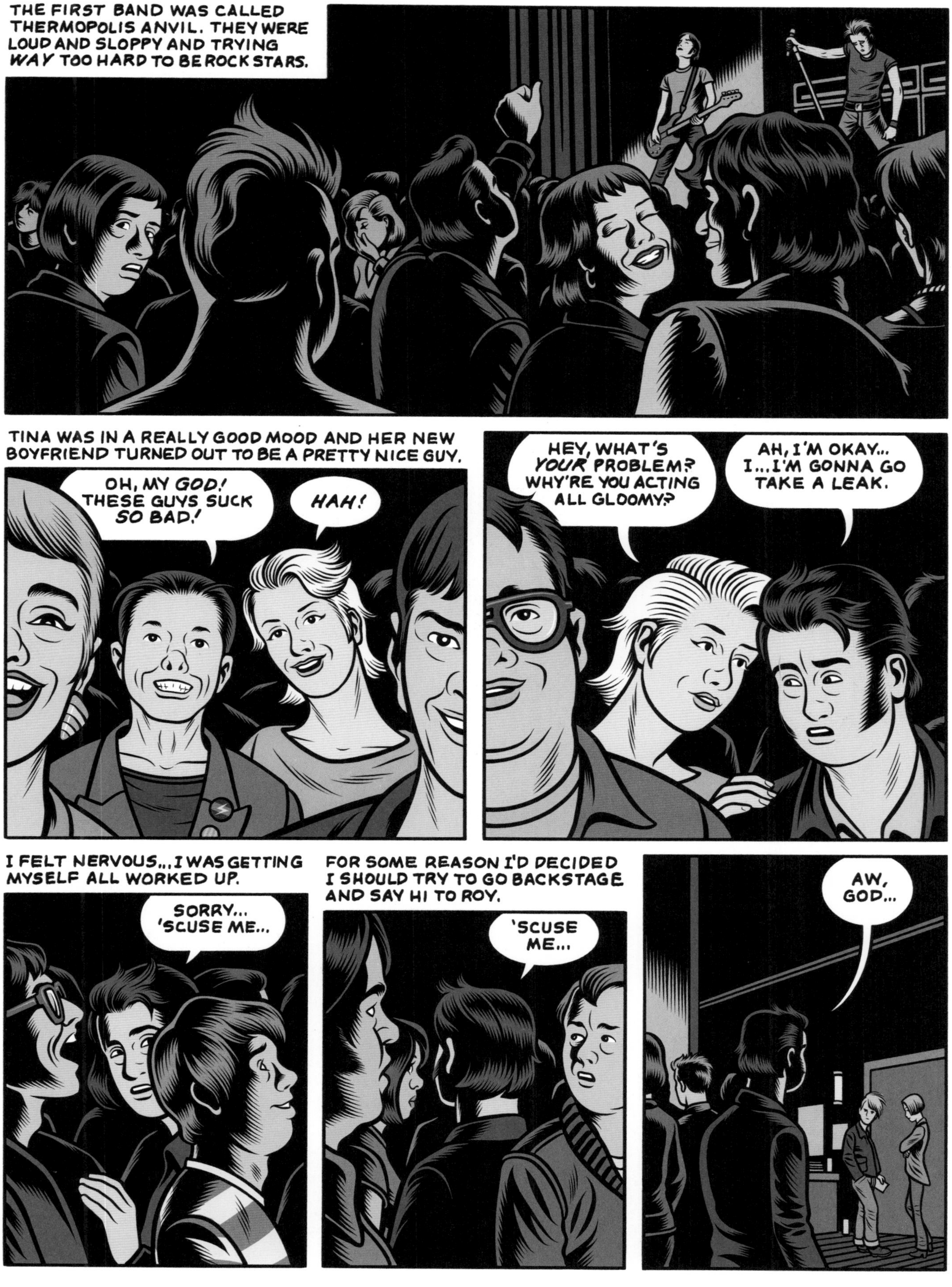
THE FIRST BAND WAS CALLED THERMOPOLIS ANVIL. THEY WERE LOUD AND SLOPPY AND TRYING WAY TOO HARD TO BE ROCK STARS.
TINA WAS IN A REALLY GOOD MOOD AND HER NEW BOYFRIEND TURNED OUT TO BE A PRETTY NICE GUY.
OH, MY GOD! THESE GUYS SUCK SO BAD!
HAH!
HEY, WHAT'S YOUR PROBLEM? WHY'RE YOU ACTING ALL GLOOMY?
AH, I'M OKAY... I...I'M GONNA GO TAKE A LEAK.
I FELT NERVOUS...I WAS GETTING MYSELF ALL WORKED UP.
SORRY... 'SCUSE ME...
FOR SOME REASON I'D DECIDED I SHOULD TRY TO GO BACKSTAGE AND SAY HI TO ROY.
'SCUSE ME...
AW, GOD...

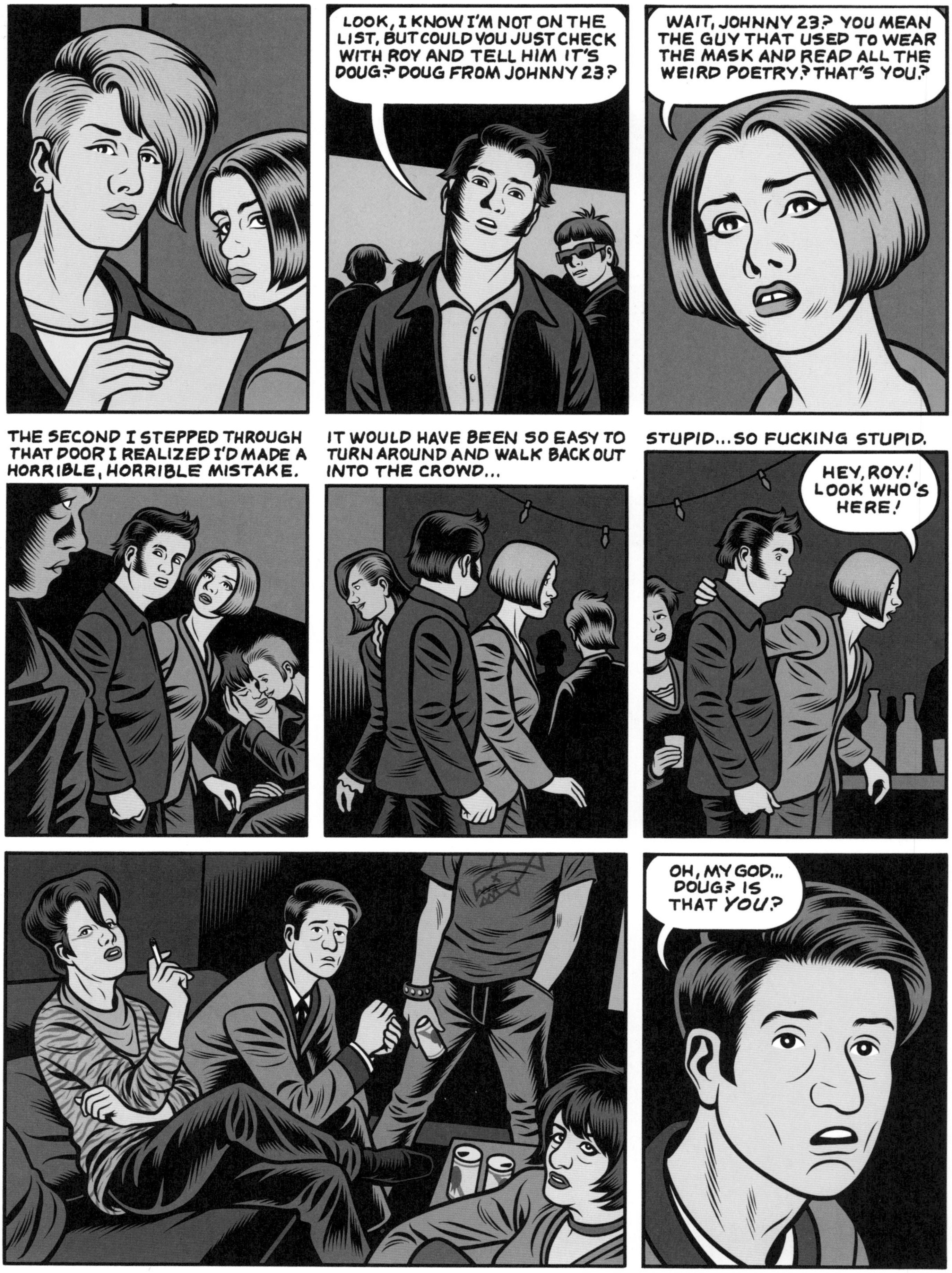
LOOK, I KNOW I'M NOT ON THE LIST, BUT COULD YOU JUST CHECK WITH ROY AND TELL HIM IT'S DOUG? DOUG FROM JOHNNY 23?
WAIT, JOHNNY 23? YOU MEAN THE GUY THAT USED TO WEAR THE MASK AND READ ALL THE WEIRD POETRY? THAT'S YOU?
THE SECOND I STEPPED THROUGH THAT DOOR I REALIZED I'D MADE A HORRIBLE, HORRIBLE MISTAKE.
IT WOULD HAVE BEEN SO EASY TO TURN AROUND AND WALK BACK OUT INTO THE CROWD...
STUPID... SO FUCKING STUPID.
HEY, ROY! LOOK WHO'S HERE!
OH, MY GOD... DOUG? IS THAT YOU?

ROY DIDN'T INTRODUCE ME TO ANYONE BUT HE SEEMED HAPPY TO SEE ME...CURIOUS ABOUT WHAT I'D BEEN DOING WITH MY LIFE FOR THE PAST FEW YEARS.

...AND I WORK AT THIS AMAZING RECORD STORE CALLED CELLOPHANE SQUARE...YOU'D *LOVE* IT!

...AND I'VE KEPT UP WITH ALL YOUR RECORDS...THE EARLY SINGLES, EXTENDED MIXES... EVEN JAPANESE IMPORTS.

I KEPT RAMBLING ON AND ON AND AFTER A WHILE I NOTICED HE WAS STARING OVER MY SHOULDER.

I STILL TAKE A FEW PHOTOS AND UH...UH...

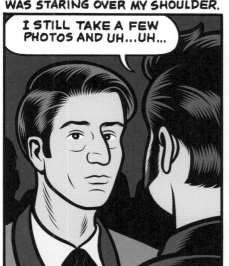

...STARING AT SOMEONE LEANING UP AGAINST THE WALL BEHIND ME.

HEY, *NICKY!* COME HERE, IT'S *DOUG!*

I KNOW WHO IT IS...AND I'VE GOT NOTHIN' TO SAY TO HIM.

AW MAN...SORRY ABOUT THAT, AND...LOOK, I GOTTA GO GET READY FOR THE SHOW, BUT IT WAS GREAT SEEING YOU!

SURE, I UNDERSTAND. I...I'LL SEE YOU LATER.

HEY, IT'S TIME FOR YOU TO GO. NOBODY WANTS YOU HERE.

GO ON, GET *OUT* OF HERE! GO!

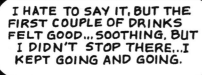
I DIDN'T EVEN BOTHER TO TELL TINA I WAS LEAVING.

I JUST WALKED OUT AND LOOKED FOR THE NEAREST BAR.

I HATE TO SAY IT, BUT THE FIRST COUPLE OF DRINKS FELT GOOD...SOOTHING, BUT I DIDN'T STOP THERE...I KEPT GOING AND GOING.

AFTER A WHILE, I... SALLY? SWEETHEART? ARE YOU STILL AWAKE?

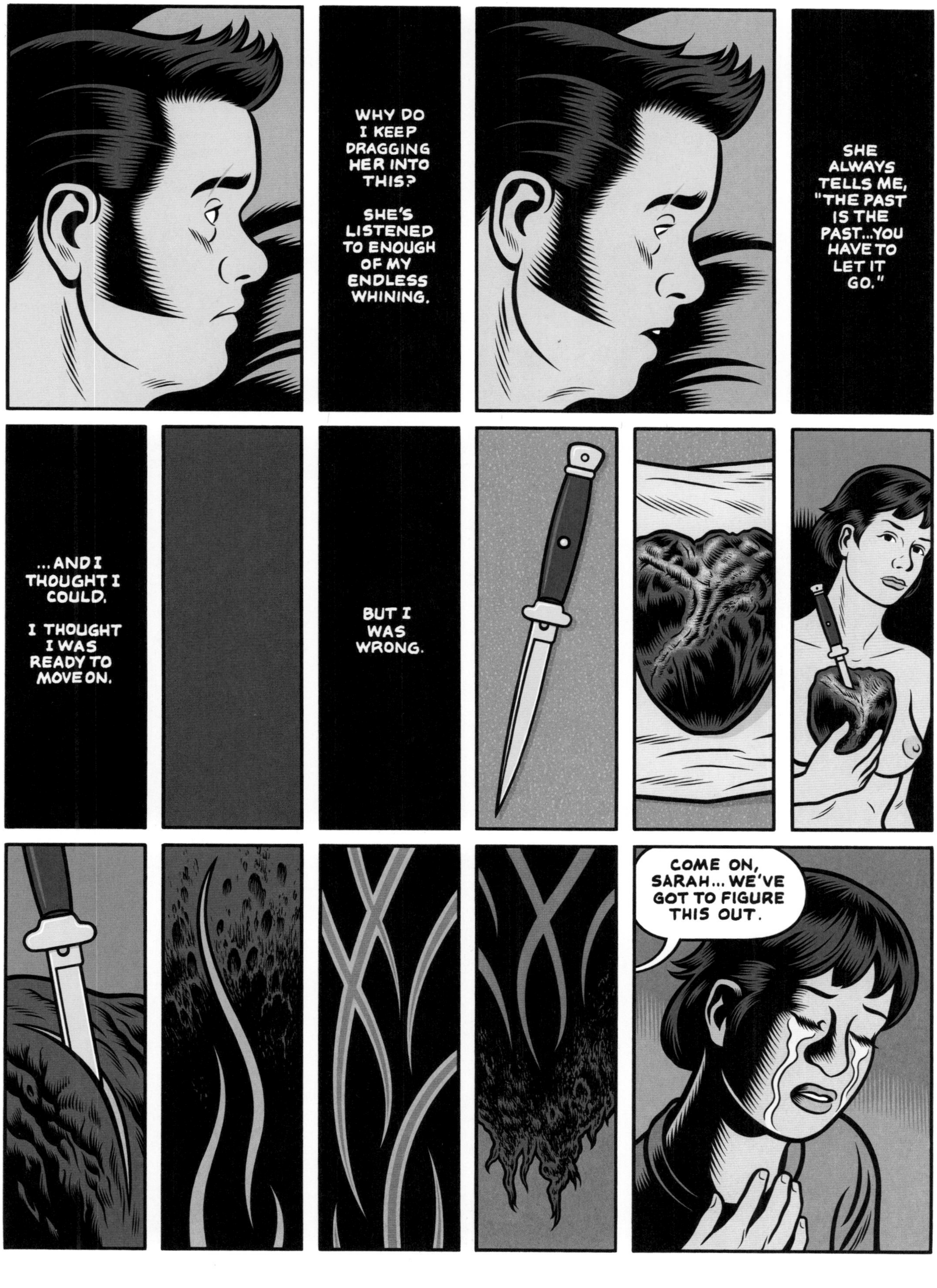
WHY DO I KEEP DRAGGING HER INTO THIS?
SHE'S LISTENED TO ENOUGH OF MY ENDLESS WHINING.
SHE ALWAYS TELLS ME, "THE PAST IS THE PAST...YOU HAVE TO LET IT GO."
...AND I THOUGHT I COULD.
I THOUGHT I WAS READY TO MOVE ON.
BUT I WAS WRONG.
COME ON, SARAH... WE'VE GOT TO FIGURE THIS OUT.

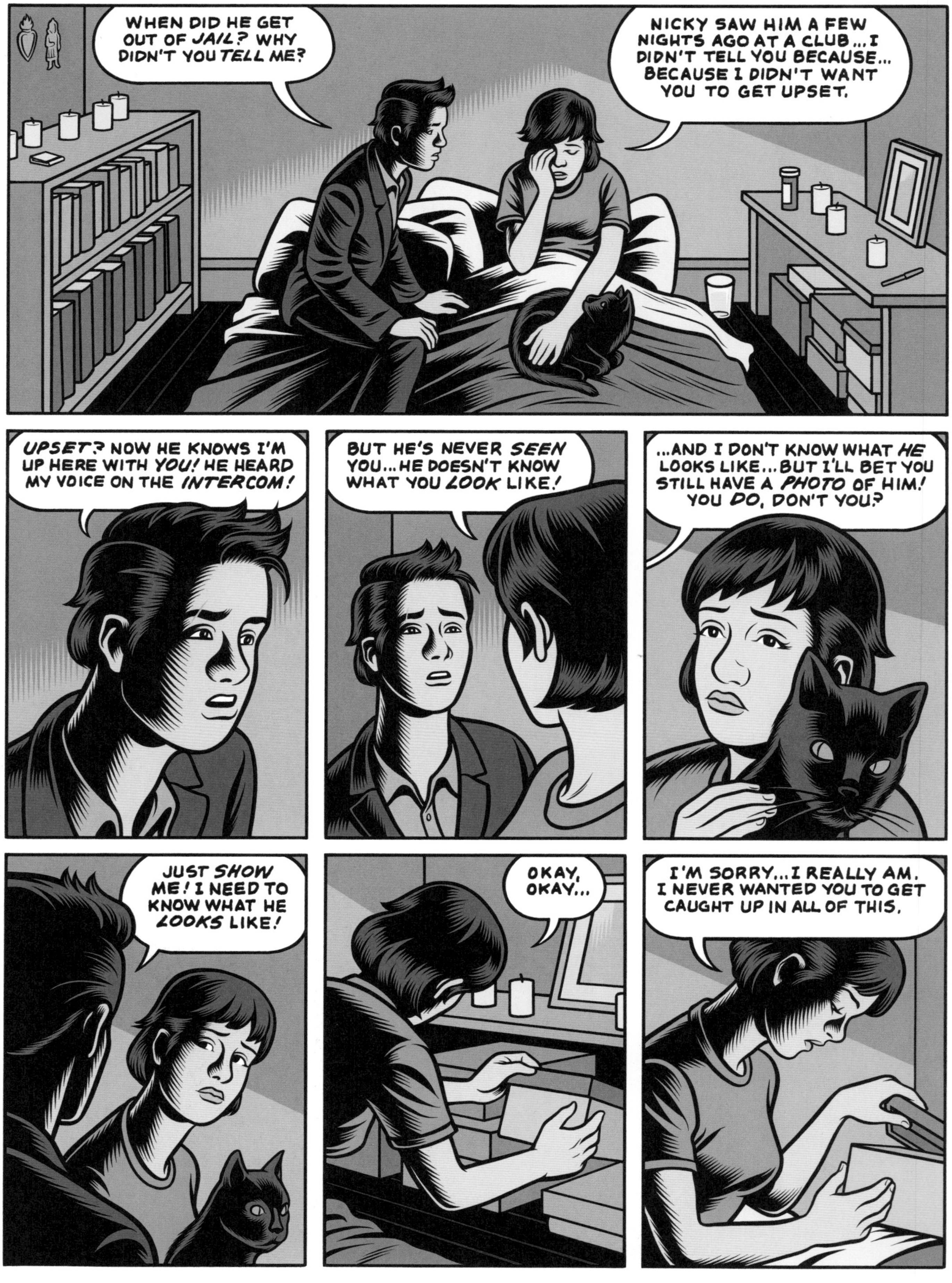
WHEN DID HE GET OUT OF JAIL? WHY DIDN'T YOU TELL ME?
NICKY SAW HIM A FEW NIGHTS AGO AT A CLUB... I DIDN'T TELL YOU BECAUSE... BECAUSE I DIDN'T WANT YOU TO GET UPSET.
UPSET? NOW HE KNOWS I'M UP HERE WITH YOU! HE HEARD MY VOICE ON THE INTERCOM!
BUT HE'S NEVER SEEN YOU... HE DOESN'T KNOW WHAT YOU LOOK LIKE!
...AND I DON'T KNOW WHAT HE LOOKS LIKE... BUT I'LL BET YOU STILL HAVE A PHOTO OF HIM! YOU DO, DON'T YOU?
JUST SHOW ME! I NEED TO KNOW WHAT HE LOOKS LIKE!
OKAY, OKAY...
I'M SORRY... I REALLY AM. I NEVER WANTED YOU TO GET CAUGHT UP IN ALL OF THIS.

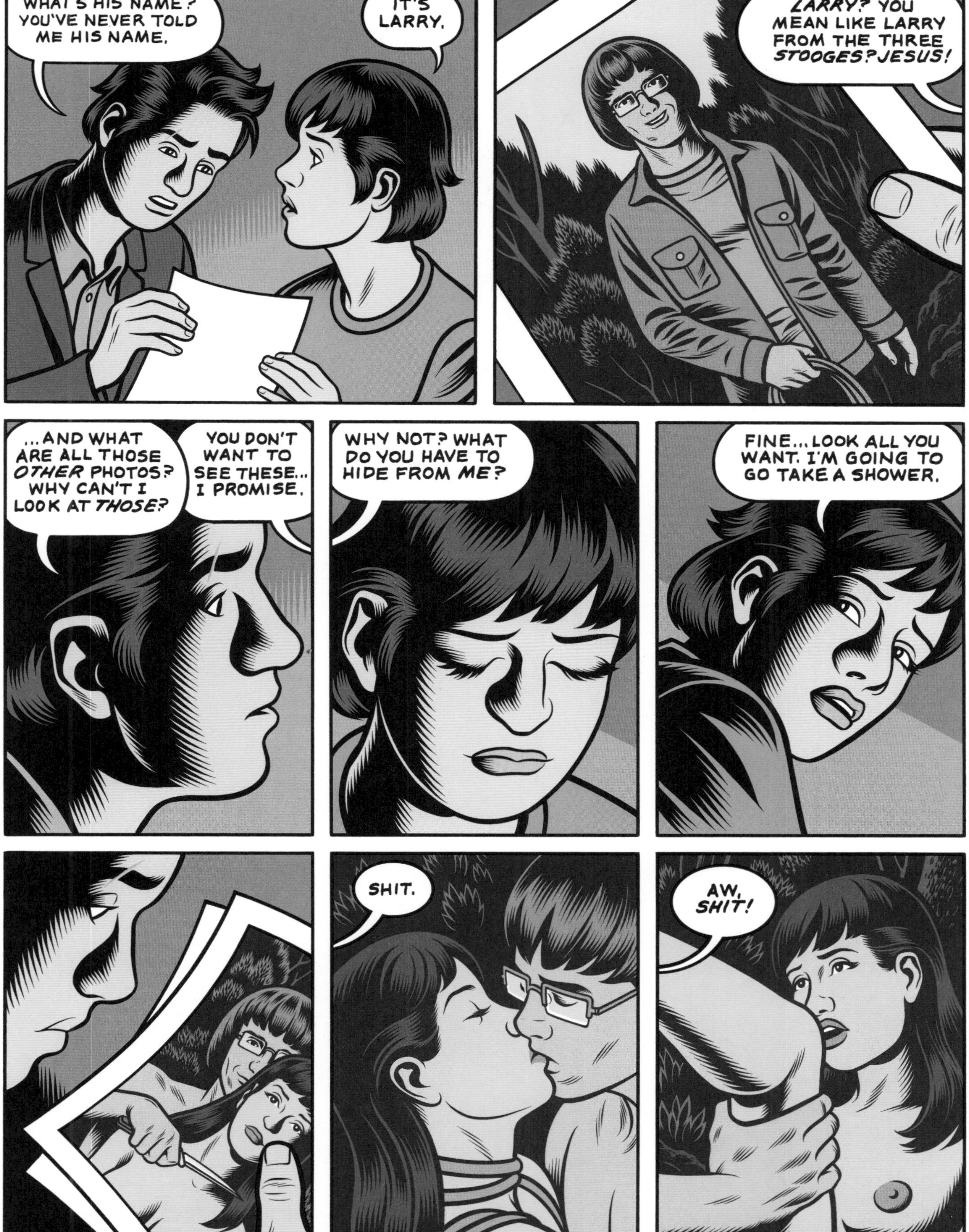
WHAT'S HIS NAME? YOU'VE NEVER TOLD ME HIS NAME.
IT'S LARRY.
LARRY? YOU MEAN LIKE LARRY FROM THE THREE STOOGES? JESUS!
...AND WHAT ARE ALL THOSE OTHER PHOTOS? WHY CAN'T I LOOK AT THOSE?
YOU DON'T WANT TO SEE THESE... I PROMISE.
WHY NOT? WHAT DO YOU HAVE TO HIDE FROM ME?
FINE... LOOK ALL YOU WANT. I'M GOING TO GO TAKE A SHOWER.
SHIT.
AW, SHIT!

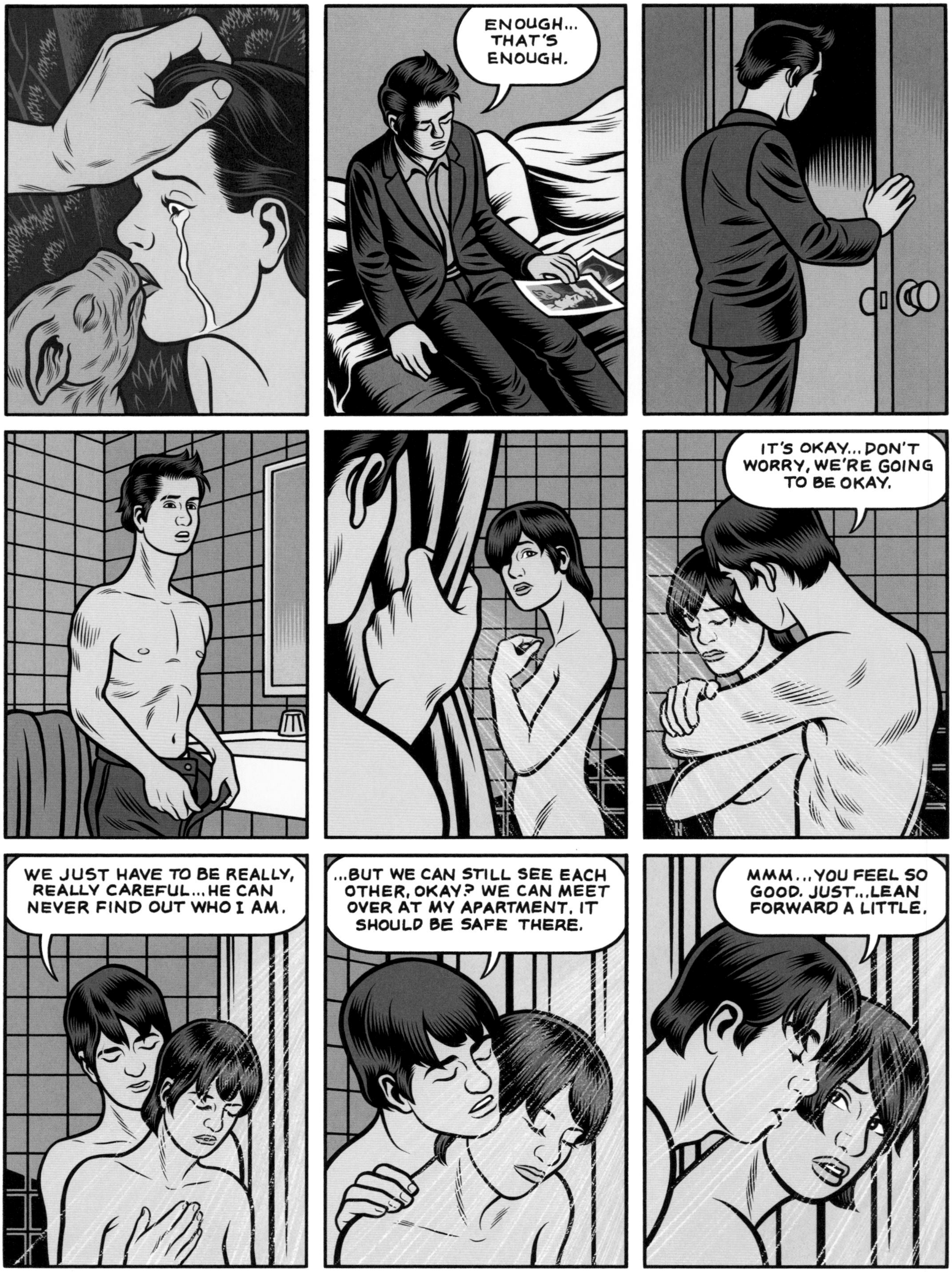
ENOUGH... THAT'S ENOUGH.
IT'S OKAY... DON'T WORRY, WE'RE GOING TO BE OKAY.
WE JUST HAVE TO BE REALLY, REALLY CAREFUL... HE CAN NEVER FIND OUT WHO I AM.
...BUT WE CAN STILL SEE EACH OTHER, OKAY? WE CAN MEET OVER AT MY APARTMENT. IT SHOULD BE SAFE THERE.
MMM... YOU FEEL SO GOOD. JUST...LEAN FORWARD A LITTLE.

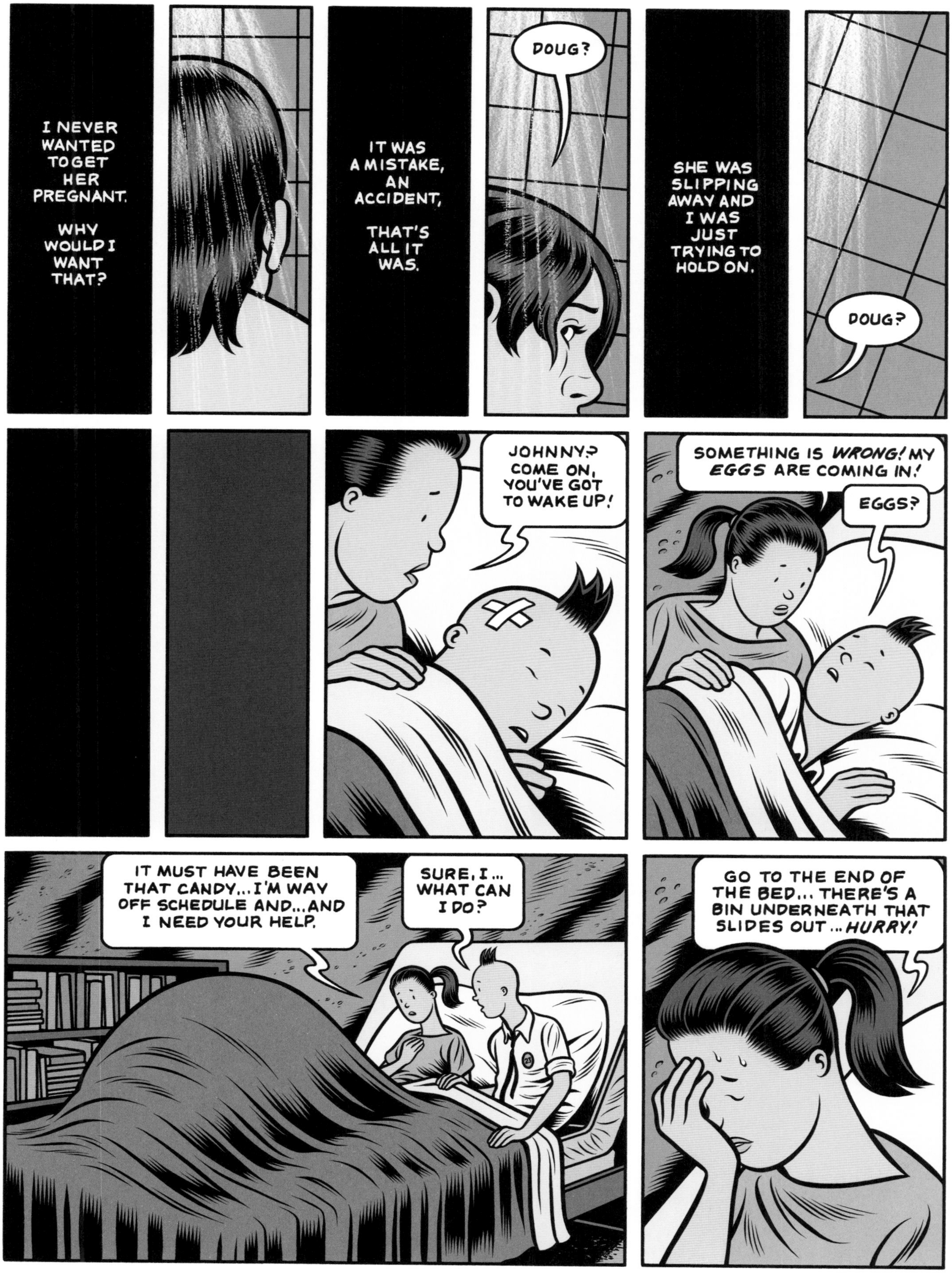

I NEVER WANTED TO GET HER PREGNANT.
WHY WOULD I WANT THAT?
IT WAS A MISTAKE, AN ACCIDENT,
THAT'S ALL IT WAS.
DOUG?
SHE WAS SLIPPING AWAY AND I WAS JUST TRYING TO HOLD ON.
DOUG?
JOHNNY? COME ON, YOU'VE GOT TO WAKE UP!
SOMETHING IS WRONG! MY EGGS ARE COMING IN!
EGGS?
IT MUST HAVE BEEN THAT CANDY... I'M WAY OFF SCHEDULE AND... AND I NEED YOUR HELP.
SURE, I... WHAT CAN I DO?
GO TO THE END OF THE BED... THERE'S A BIN UNDERNEATH THAT SLIDES OUT... HURRY!

YOU CAN PUSH THE BIN OFF TO THE SIDE... THAT'S WHERE YOU'LL LOAD UP THE EGGS.
NOW PULL BACK THE COVERS AND GET READY... THE FIRST ONE'S COMING!
READY? IT'S COMING!
UNN...
AHHH!
CRACK!

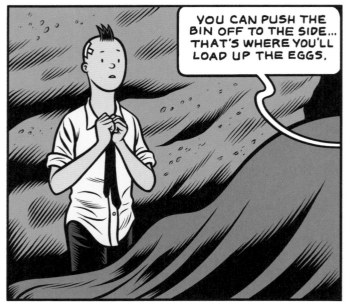

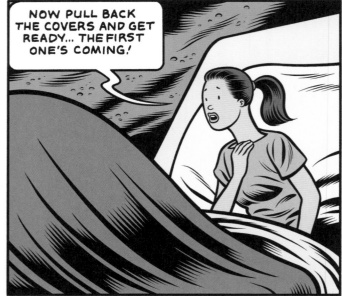

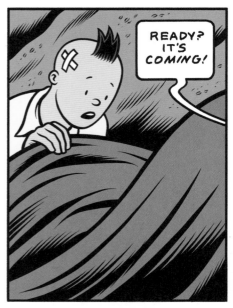

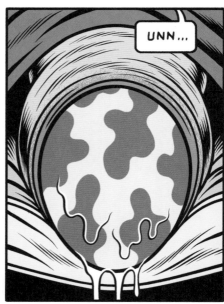

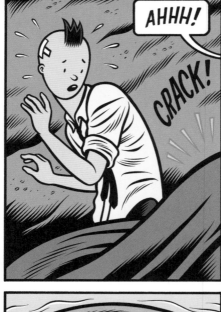

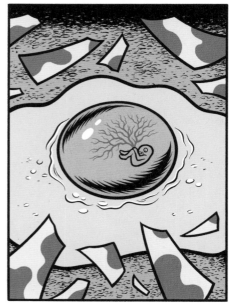

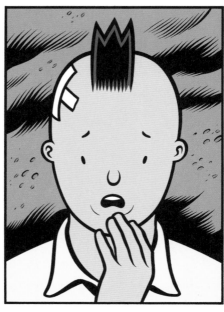

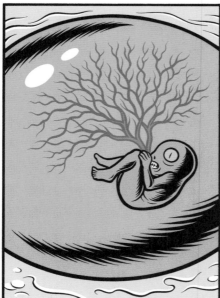

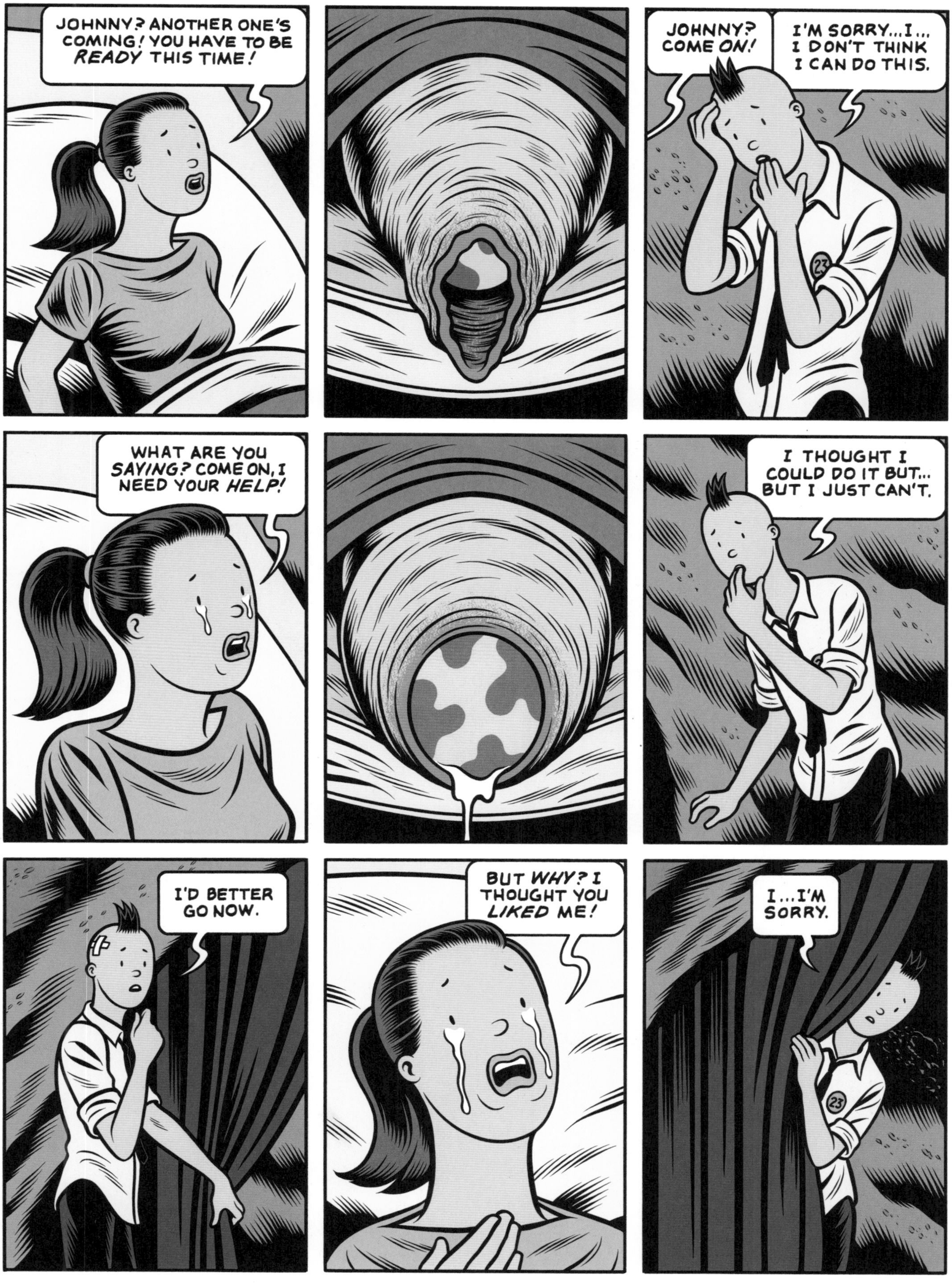
JOHNNY? ANOTHER ONE'S COMING! YOU HAVE TO BE *READY* THIS TIME!
JOHNNY? COME *ON*!
I'M SORRY...I... I DON'T THINK I CAN DO THIS.
WHAT ARE YOU *SAYING?* COME ON, I NEED YOUR *HELP!*
I THOUGHT I COULD DO IT BUT... BUT I JUST CAN'T.
I'D BETTER GO NOW.
BUT *WHY?* I THOUGHT YOU *LIKED* ME!
I...I'M SORRY.

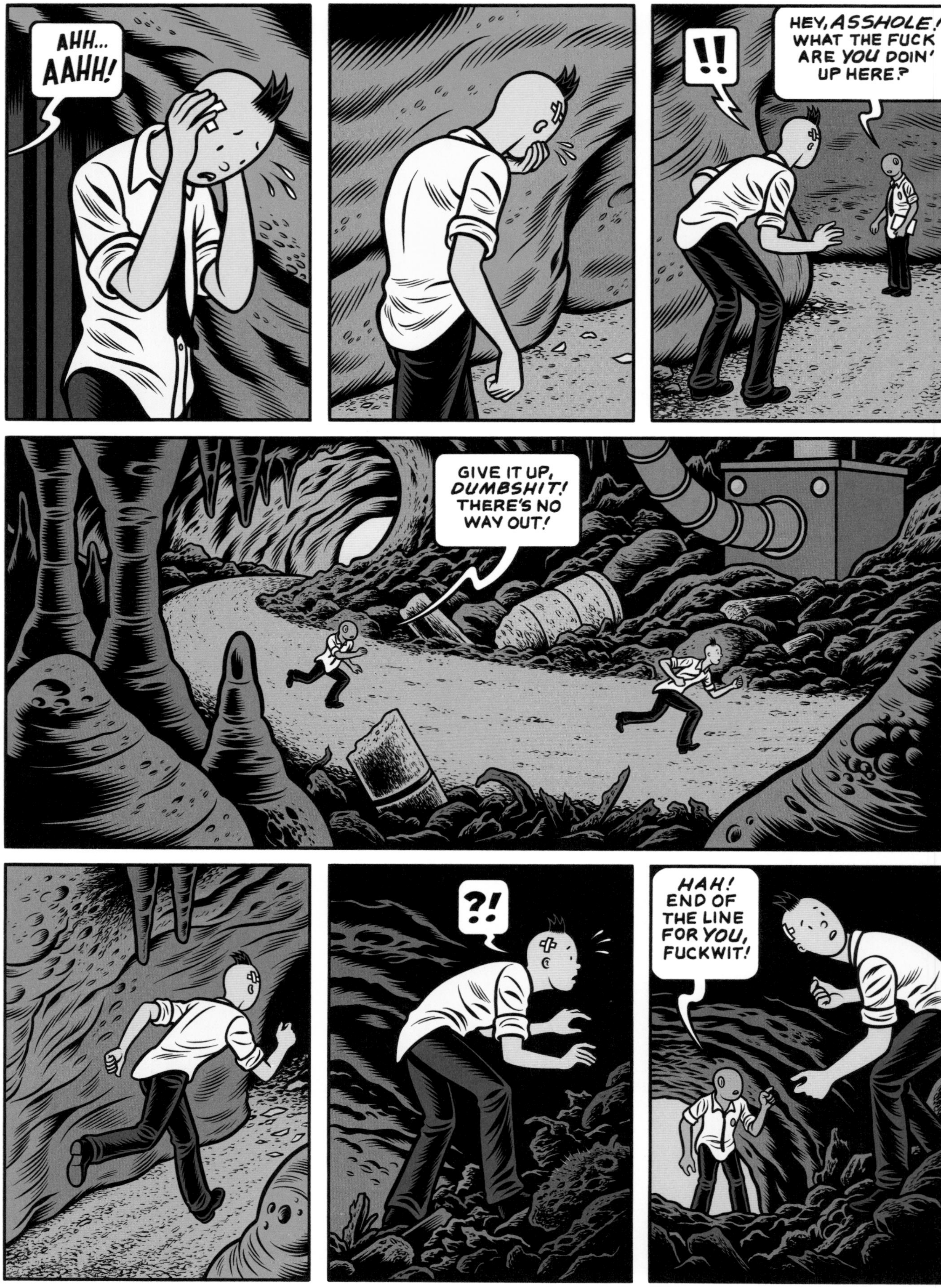
AHH... AAHH!
!!
HEY, ASSHOLE! WHAT THE FUCK ARE YOU DOIN' UP HERE?
GIVE IT UP, DUMBSHIT! THERE'S NO WAY OUT!
?!
HAH! END OF THE LINE FOR YOU, FUCKWIT!

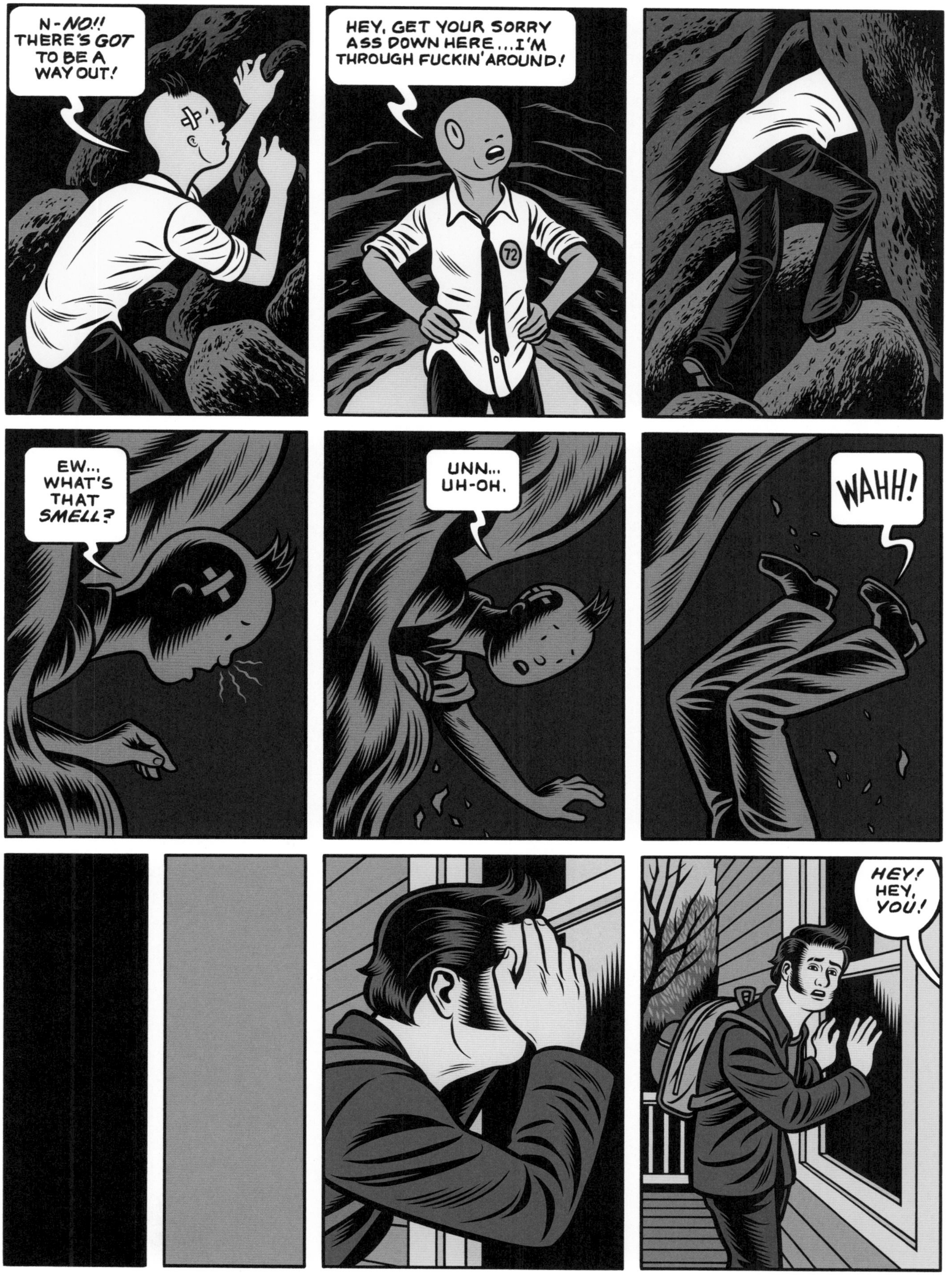
N-NO!! THERE'S GOT TO BE A WAY OUT!
HEY, GET YOUR SORRY ASS DOWN HERE...I'M THROUGH FUCKIN' AROUND!
EW... WHAT'S THAT SMELL?
UNN... UH-OH.
WAHH!
HEY! HEY, YOU!

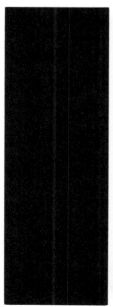

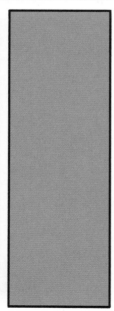

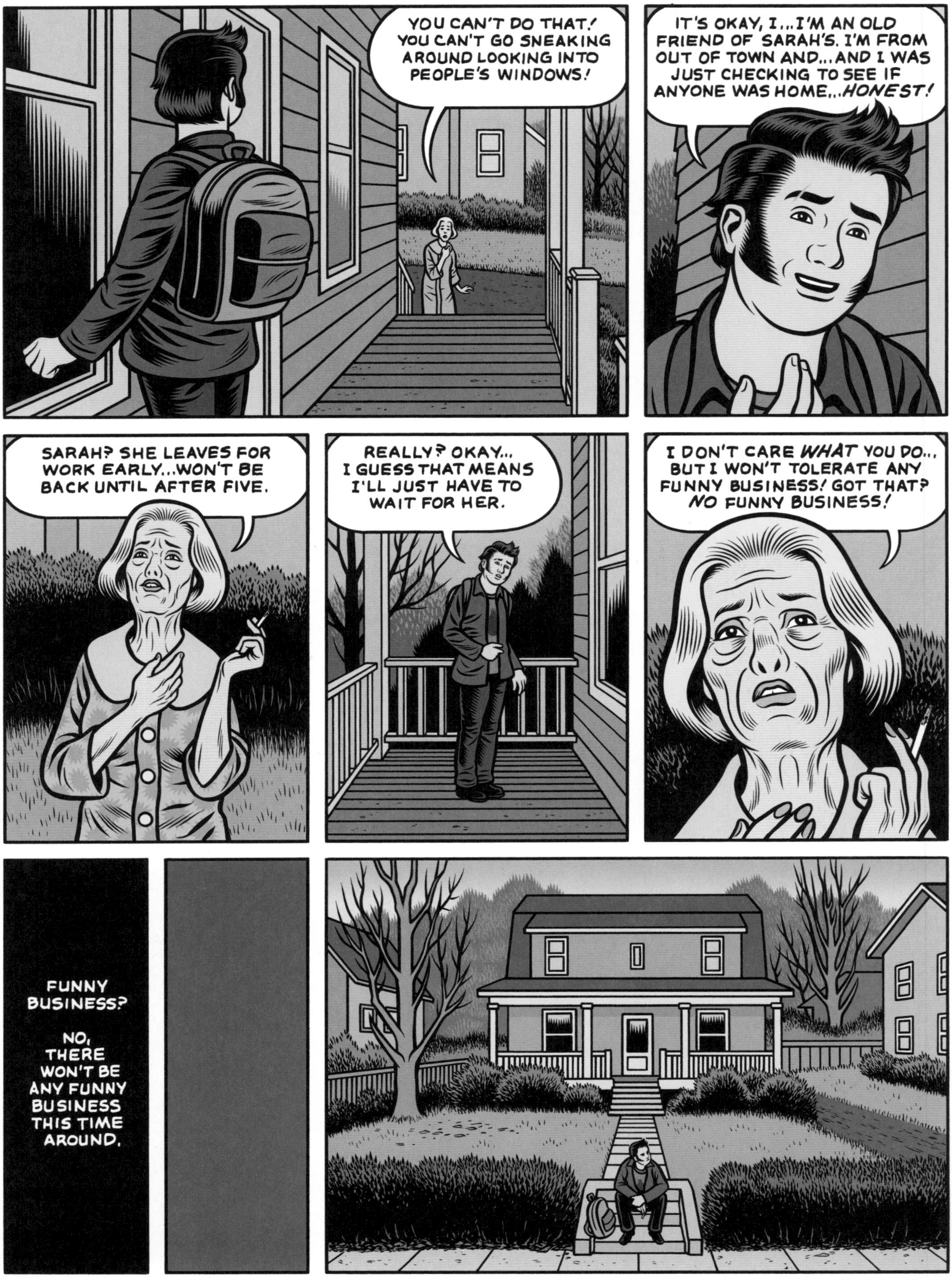

YOU CAN'T DO THAT! YOU CAN'T GO SNEAKING AROUND LOOKING INTO PEOPLE'S WINDOWS!
IT'S OKAY, I...I'M AN OLD FRIEND OF SARAH'S. I'M FROM OUT OF TOWN AND...AND I WAS JUST CHECKING TO SEE IF ANYONE WAS HOME...HONEST!
SARAH? SHE LEAVES FOR WORK EARLY...WON'T BE BACK UNTIL AFTER FIVE.
REALLY? OKAY... I GUESS THAT MEANS I'LL JUST HAVE TO WAIT FOR HER.
I DON'T CARE WHAT YOU DO... BUT I WON'T TOLERATE ANY FUNNY BUSINESS! GOT THAT? NO FUNNY BUSINESS!
FUNNY BUSINESS?
NO, THERE WON'T BE ANY FUNNY BUSINESS THIS TIME AROUND.

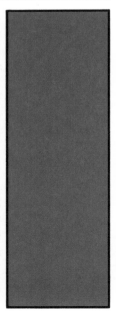

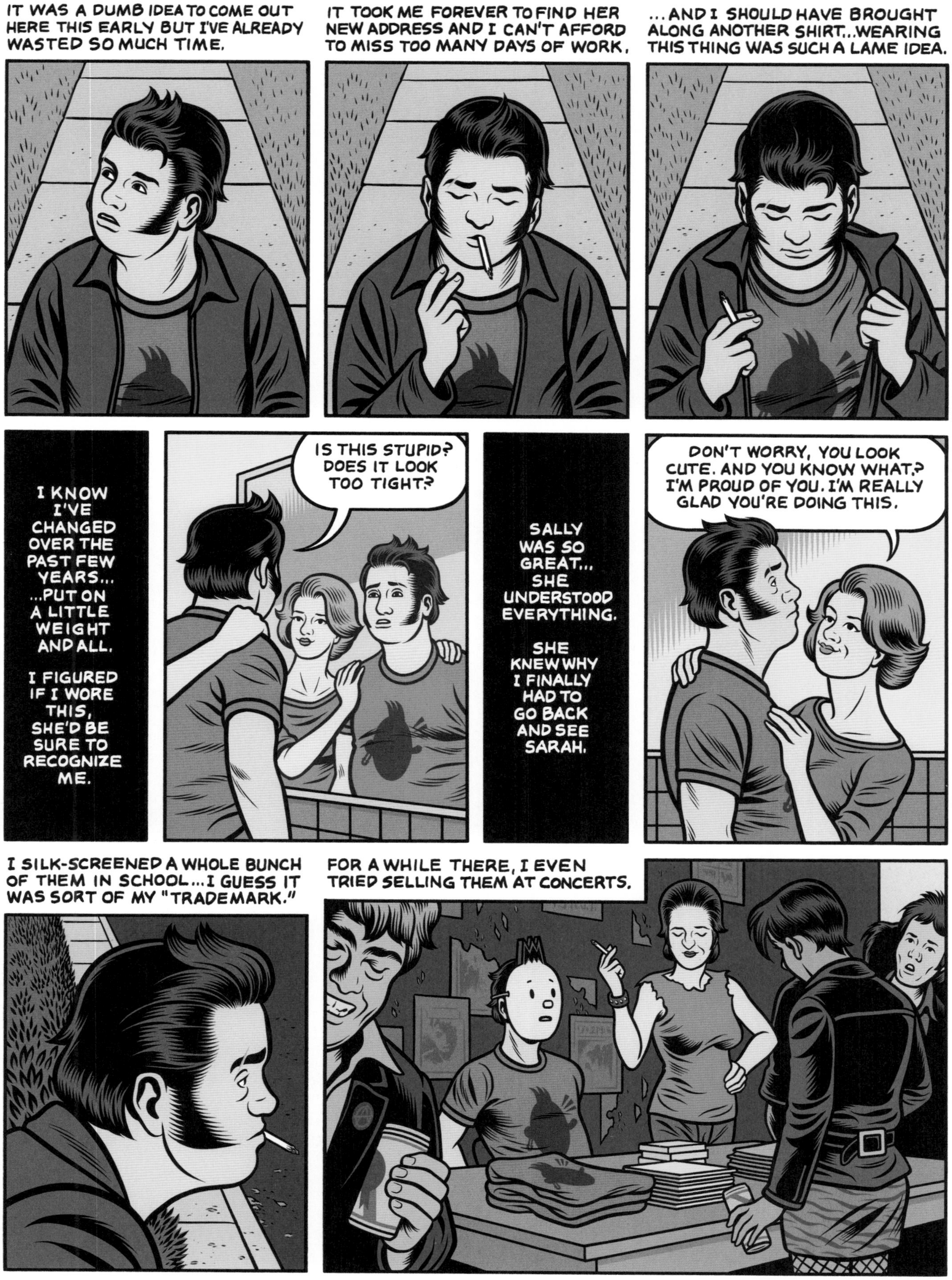
IT WAS A DUMB IDEA TO COME OUT HERE THIS EARLY BUT I'VE ALREADY WASTED SO MUCH TIME.
IT TOOK ME FOREVER TO FIND HER NEW ADDRESS AND I CAN'T AFFORD TO MISS TOO MANY DAYS OF WORK.
...AND I SHOULD HAVE BROUGHT ALONG ANOTHER SHIRT...WEARING THIS THING WAS SUCH A LAME IDEA.
I KNOW I'VE CHANGED OVER THE PAST FEW YEARS... ...PUT ON A LITTLE WEIGHT AND ALL.
I FIGURED IF I WORE THIS, SHE'D BE SURE TO RECOGNIZE ME.
IS THIS STUPID? DOES IT LOOK TOO TIGHT?
SALLY WAS SO GREAT... SHE UNDERSTOOD EVERYTHING.
SHE KNEW WHY I FINALLY HAD TO GO BACK AND SEE SARAH.
DON'T WORRY, YOU LOOK CUTE. AND YOU KNOW WHAT? I'M PROUD OF YOU. I'M REALLY GLAD YOU'RE DOING THIS.
I SILK-SCREENED A WHOLE BUNCH OF THEM IN SCHOOL...I GUESS IT WAS SORT OF MY "TRADEMARK."
FOR A WHILE THERE, I EVEN TRIED SELLING THEM AT CONCERTS.

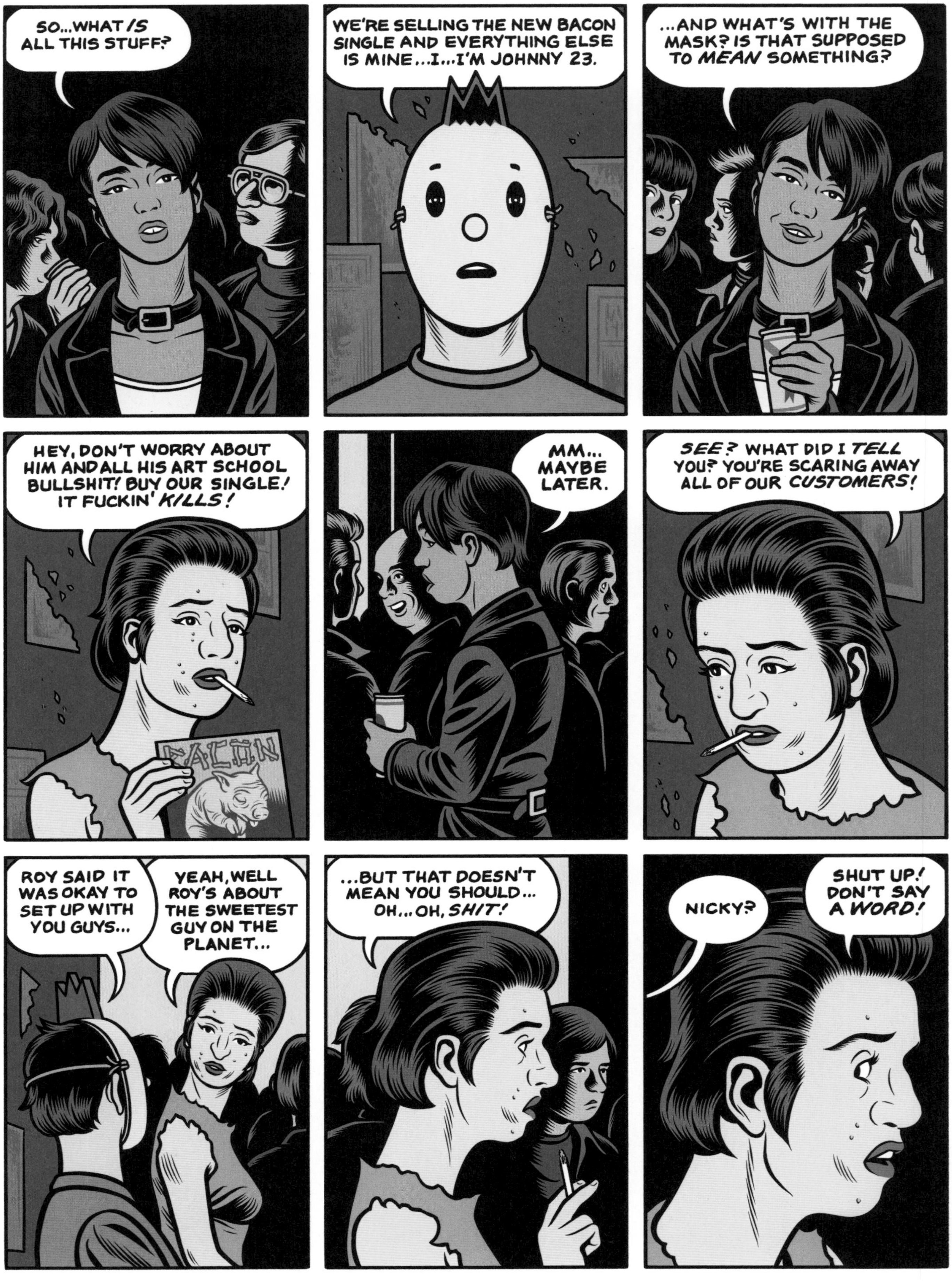
SO...WHAT IS ALL THIS STUFF?
WE'RE SELLING THE NEW BACON SINGLE AND EVERYTHING ELSE IS MINE...I...I'M JOHNNY 23.
...AND WHAT'S WITH THE MASK? IS THAT SUPPOSED TO MEAN SOMETHING?
HEY, DON'T WORRY ABOUT HIM AND ALL HIS ART SCHOOL BULLSHIT! BUY OUR SINGLE! IT FUCKIN' KILLS!
BACON
MM... MAYBE LATER.
SEE? WHAT DID I TELL YOU? YOU'RE SCARING AWAY ALL OF OUR CUSTOMERS!
ROY SAID IT WAS OKAY TO SET UP WITH YOU GUYS...
YEAH, WELL ROY'S ABOUT THE SWEETEST GUY ON THE PLANET...
...BUT THAT DOESN'T MEAN YOU SHOULD... OH...OH, SHIT!
NICKY?
SHUT UP! DON'T SAY A WORD!

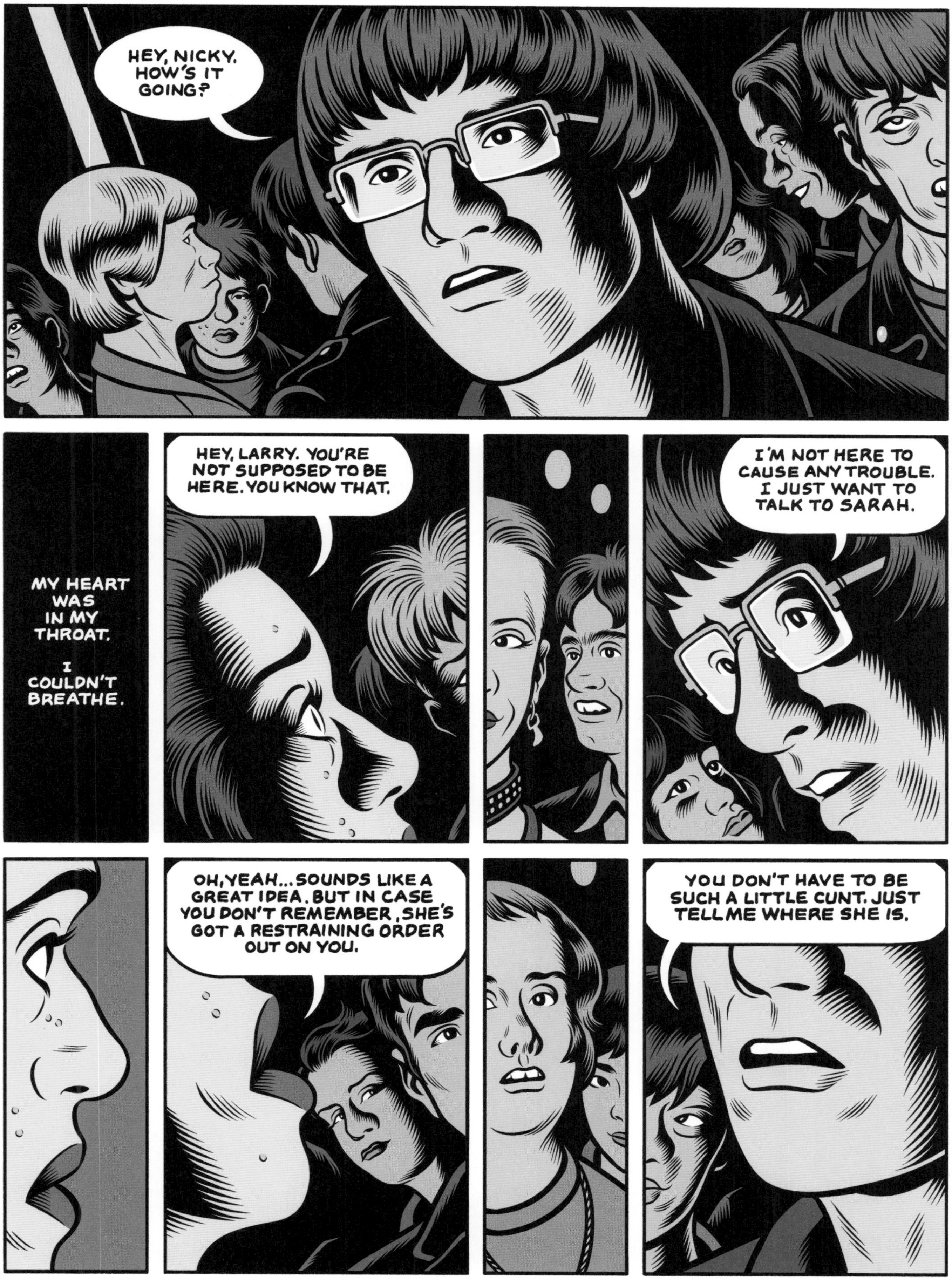
HEY, NICKY. HOW'S IT GOING?
MY HEART WAS IN MY THROAT.
I COULDN'T BREATHE.
HEY, LARRY. YOU'RE NOT SUPPOSED TO BE HERE. YOU KNOW THAT.
I'M NOT HERE TO CAUSE ANY TROUBLE. I JUST WANT TO TALK TO SARAH.
OH, YEAH... SOUNDS LIKE A GREAT IDEA. BUT IN CASE YOU DON'T REMEMBER, SHE'S GOT A RESTRAINING ORDER OUT ON YOU.
YOU DON'T HAVE TO BE SUCH A LITTLE CUNT. JUST TELL ME WHERE SHE IS.

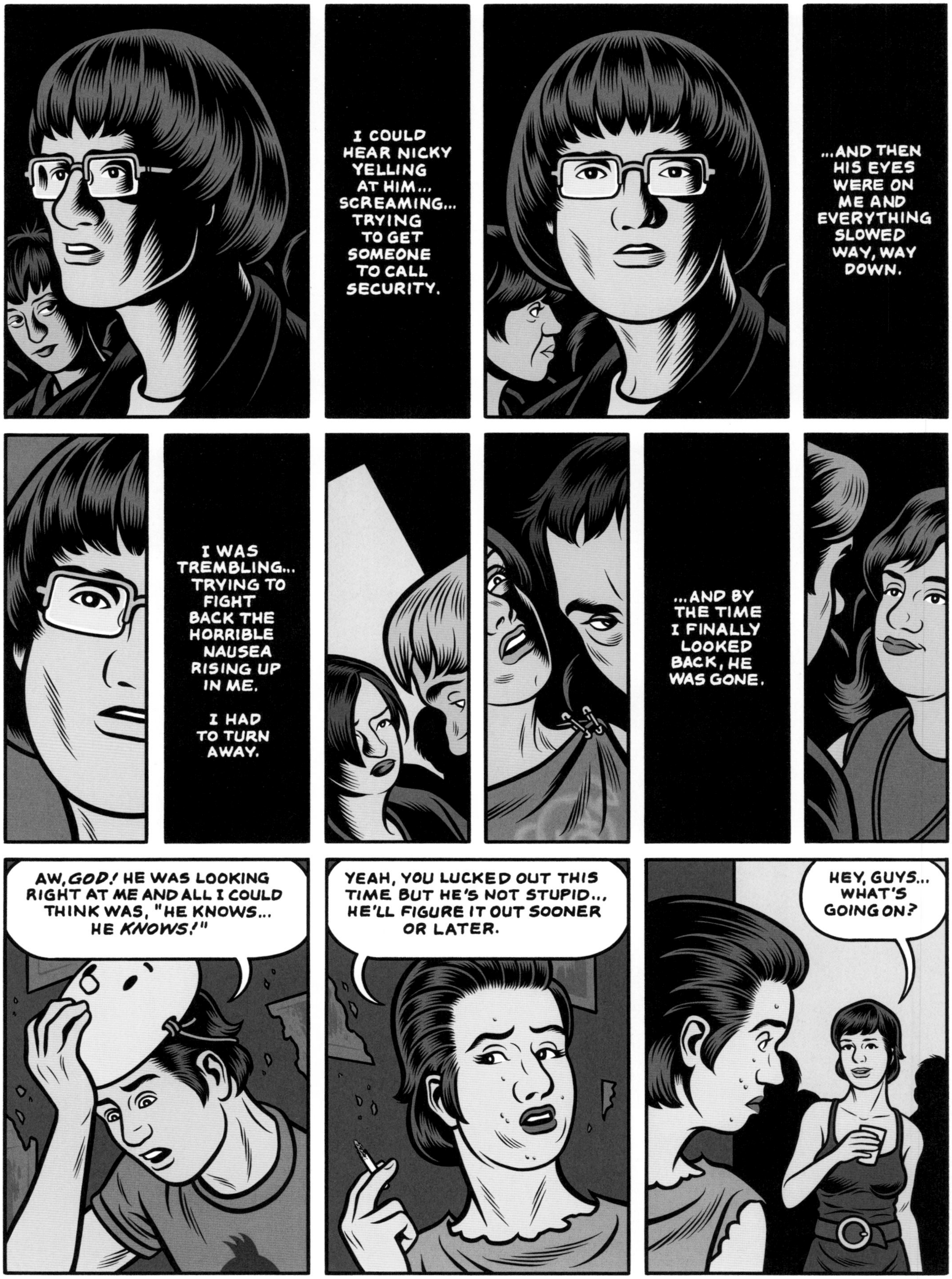
I COULD HEAR NICKY YELLING AT HIM... SCREAMING... TRYING TO GET SOMEONE TO CALL SECURITY.
...AND THEN HIS EYES WERE ON ME AND EVERYTHING SLOWED WAY, WAY DOWN.
I WAS TREMBLING... TRYING TO FIGHT BACK THE HORRIBLE NAUSEA RISING UP IN ME.
I HAD TO TURN AWAY.
...AND BY THE TIME I FINALLY LOOKED BACK, HE WAS GONE.
AW, GOD! HE WAS LOOKING RIGHT AT ME AND ALL I COULD THINK WAS, "HE KNOWS... HE KNOWS!"
YEAH, YOU LUCKED OUT THIS TIME BUT HE'S NOT STUPID... HE'LL FIGURE IT OUT SOONER OR LATER.
HEY, GUYS... WHAT'S GOING ON?

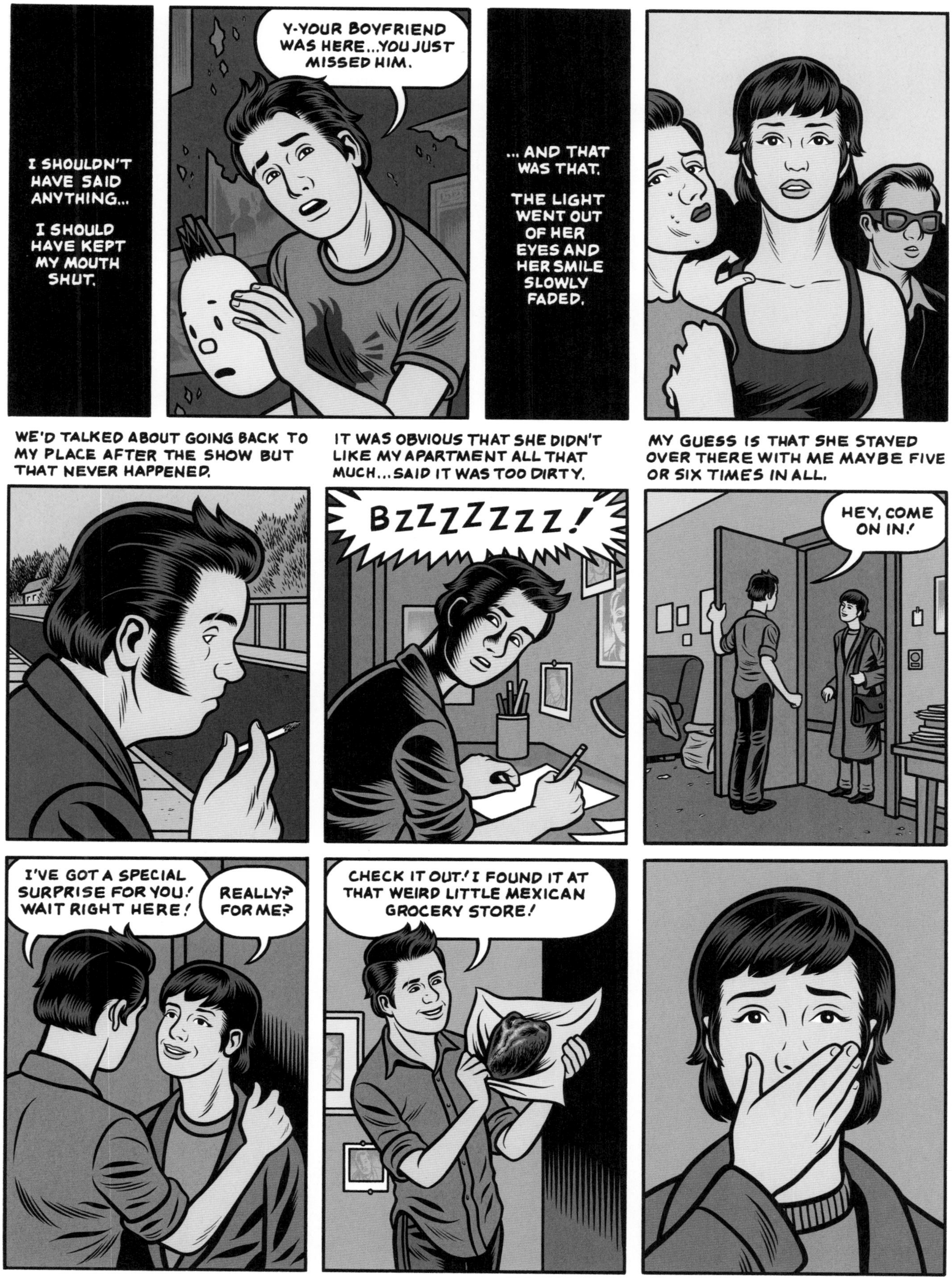
I SHOULDN'T HAVE SAID ANYTHING...
I SHOULD HAVE KEPT MY MOUTH SHUT.
Y-YOUR BOYFRIEND WAS HERE...YOU JUST MISSED HIM.
... AND THAT WAS THAT.
THE LIGHT WENT OUT OF HER EYES AND HER SMILE SLOWLY FADED.
WE'D TALKED ABOUT GOING BACK TO MY PLACE AFTER THE SHOW BUT THAT NEVER HAPPENED.
IT WAS OBVIOUS THAT SHE DIDN'T LIKE MY APARTMENT ALL THAT MUCH... SAID IT WAS TOO DIRTY.
BZZZZZZZ!
MY GUESS IS THAT SHE STAYED OVER THERE WITH ME MAYBE FIVE OR SIX TIMES IN ALL.
HEY, COME ON IN!
I'VE GOT A SPECIAL SURPRISE FOR YOU! WAIT RIGHT HERE!
REALLY? FOR ME?
CHECK IT OUT! I FOUND IT AT THAT WEIRD LITTLE MEXICAN GROCERY STORE!

YOU KNOW WHAT? YOU'RE JUST DOING THIS TO GET BACK AT ME.

WHAT? WHAT'RE YOU *TALKING* ABOUT?

YOU SAW THOSE PHOTOS OF ME AND LARRY AND EVER SINCE THEN YOU LOOK AT ME DIFFERENTLY...

THAT'S NOT *TRUE!*

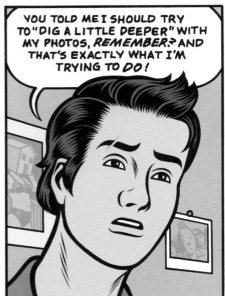

YOU TOLD ME I SHOULD TRY TO "DIG A LITTLE DEEPER" WITH MY PHOTOS, *REMEMBER*? AND THAT'S EXACTLY WHAT I'M TRYING TO *DO!*

...AND I ASKED YOU TO COME WITH ME TO MY DOCTOR'S APPOINTMENT AND YOU WERE LIKE...

HEY, I *SAID* I'D GO!

YEAH, BUT I HAD TO PRACTICALLY *FORCE* YOU INTO IT!

WE KEPT AT IT FOR HOURS...

SIFTING THROUGH THE SAME ARGUEMENTS OVER AND OVER AGAIN.

...AND I DON'T WANT TO GO THROUGH ANOTHER ABORTION, BUT I CAN'T SEE ANY OTHER WAY...

WHAT ELSE CAN YOU *DO*?

I MEAN THERE'S NO *WAY* I'D EVER BE ABLE TO BE A FATHER, YOU KNOW?

YEAH, I GET IT... LET'S JUST... LET'S DROP IT, OKAY? I'VE HAD ENOUGH FOR ONE DAY.

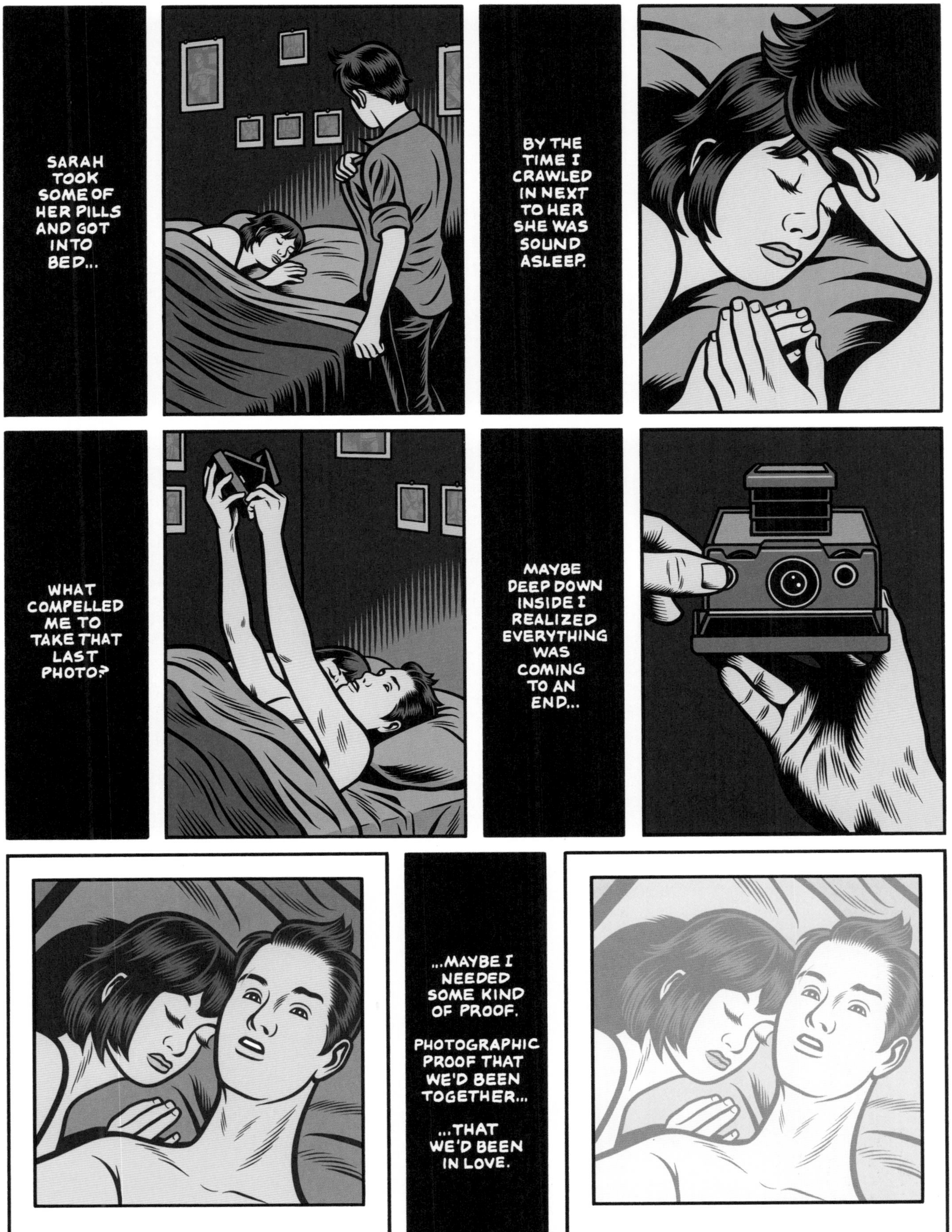
SARAH TOOK SOME OF HER PILLS AND GOT INTO BED...
BY THE TIME I CRAWLED IN NEXT TO HER SHE WAS SOUND ASLEEP.
WHAT COMPELLED ME TO TAKE THAT LAST PHOTO?
MAYBE DEEP DOWN INSIDE I REALIZED EVERYTHING WAS COMING TO AN END...
...MAYBE I NEEDED SOME KIND OF PROOF.
PHOTOGRAPHIC PROOF THAT WE'D BEEN TOGETHER...
...THAT WE'D BEEN IN LOVE.

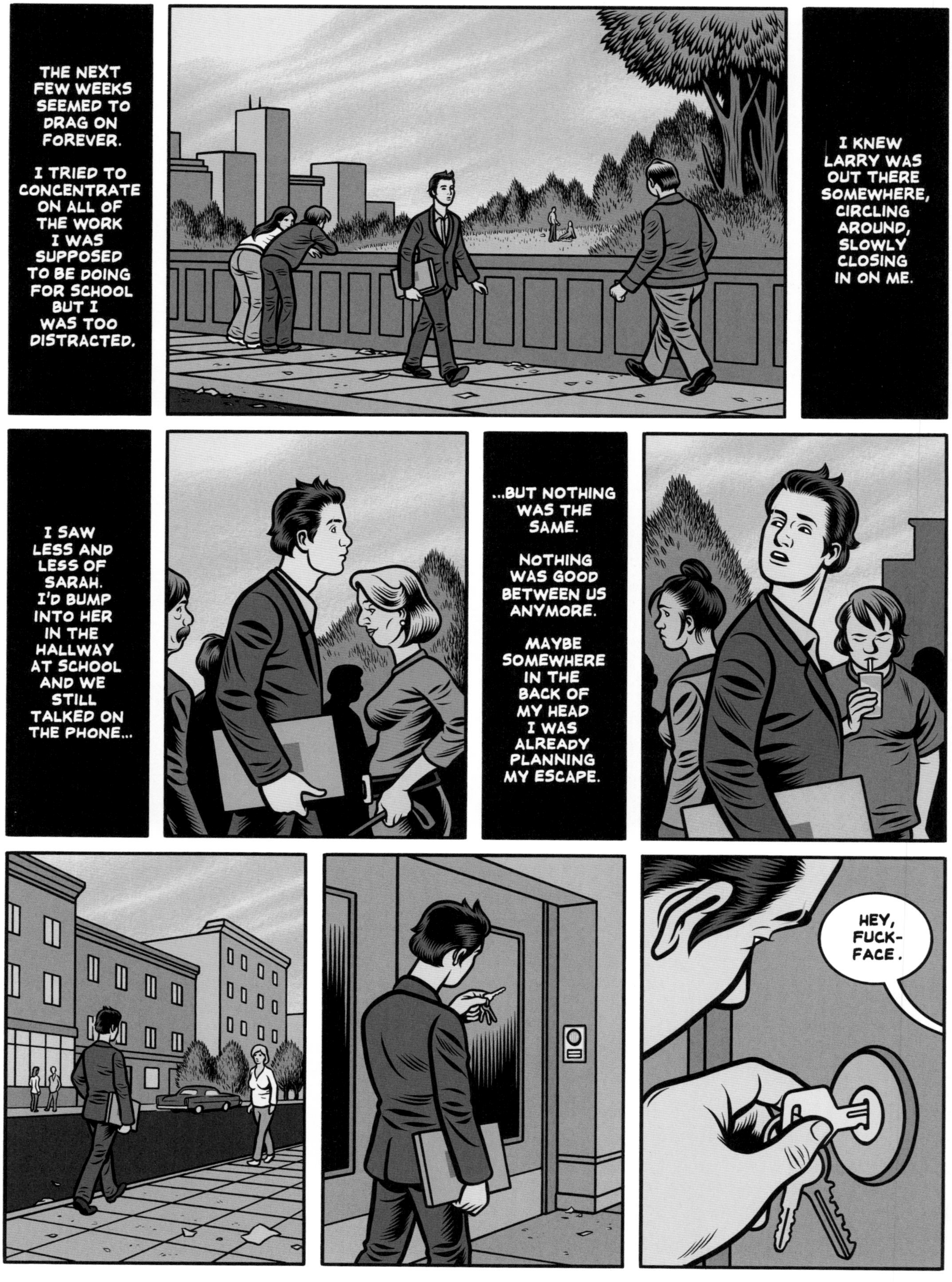
THE NEXT FEW WEEKS SEEMED TO DRAG ON FOREVER.
I TRIED TO CONCENTRATE ON ALL OF THE WORK I WAS SUPPOSED TO BE DOING FOR SCHOOL BUT I WAS TOO DISTRACTED.
I KNEW LARRY WAS OUT THERE SOMEWHERE, CIRCLING AROUND, SLOWLY CLOSING IN ON ME.
I SAW LESS AND LESS OF SARAH. I'D BUMP INTO HER IN THE HALLWAY AT SCHOOL AND WE STILL TALKED ON THE PHONE...
...BUT NOTHING WAS THE SAME.
NOTHING WAS GOOD BETWEEN US ANYMORE.
MAYBE SOMEWHERE IN THE BACK OF MY HEAD I WAS ALREADY PLANNING MY ESCAPE.
HEY, FUCK-FACE.

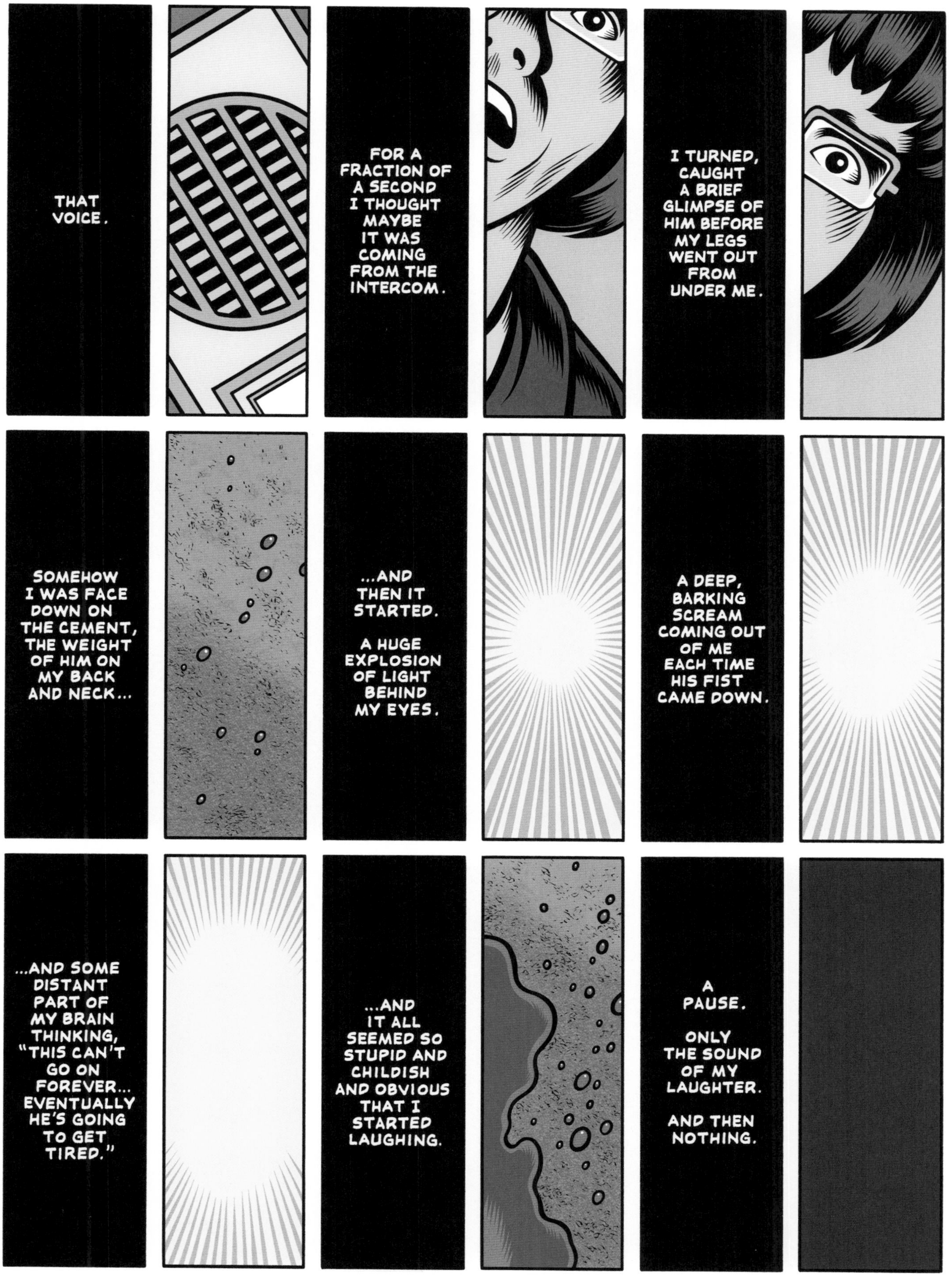
THAT VOICE.
FOR A FRACTION OF A SECOND I THOUGHT MAYBE IT WAS COMING FROM THE INTERCOM.
I TURNED, CAUGHT A BRIEF GLIMPSE OF HIM BEFORE MY LEGS WENT OUT FROM UNDER ME.
SOMEHOW I WAS FACE DOWN ON THE CEMENT, THE WEIGHT OF HIM ON MY BACK AND NECK...
...AND THEN IT STARTED.
A HUGE EXPLOSION OF LIGHT BEHIND MY EYES.
A DEEP, BARKING SCREAM COMING OUT OF ME EACH TIME HIS FIST CAME DOWN.
...AND SOME DISTANT PART OF MY BRAIN THINKING, "THIS CAN'T GO ON FOREVER... EVENTUALLY HE'S GOING TO GET TIRED."
...AND IT ALL SEEMED SO STUPID AND CHILDISH AND OBVIOUS THAT I STARTED LAUGHING.
A PAUSE.
ONLY THE SOUND OF MY LAUGHTER.
AND THEN NOTHING.

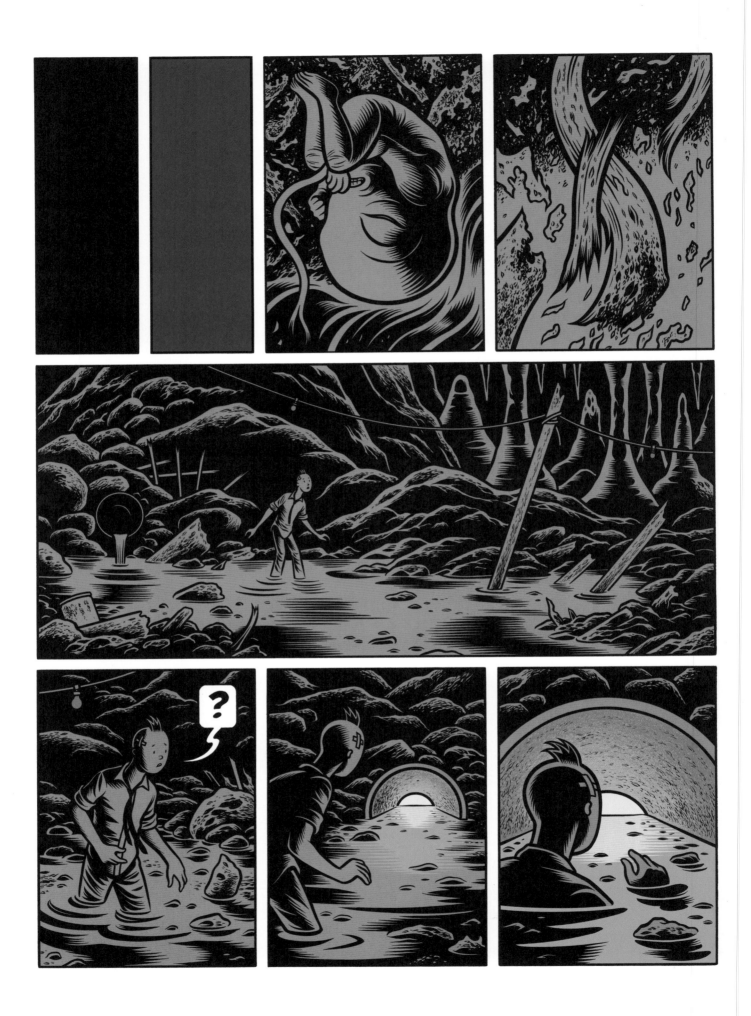

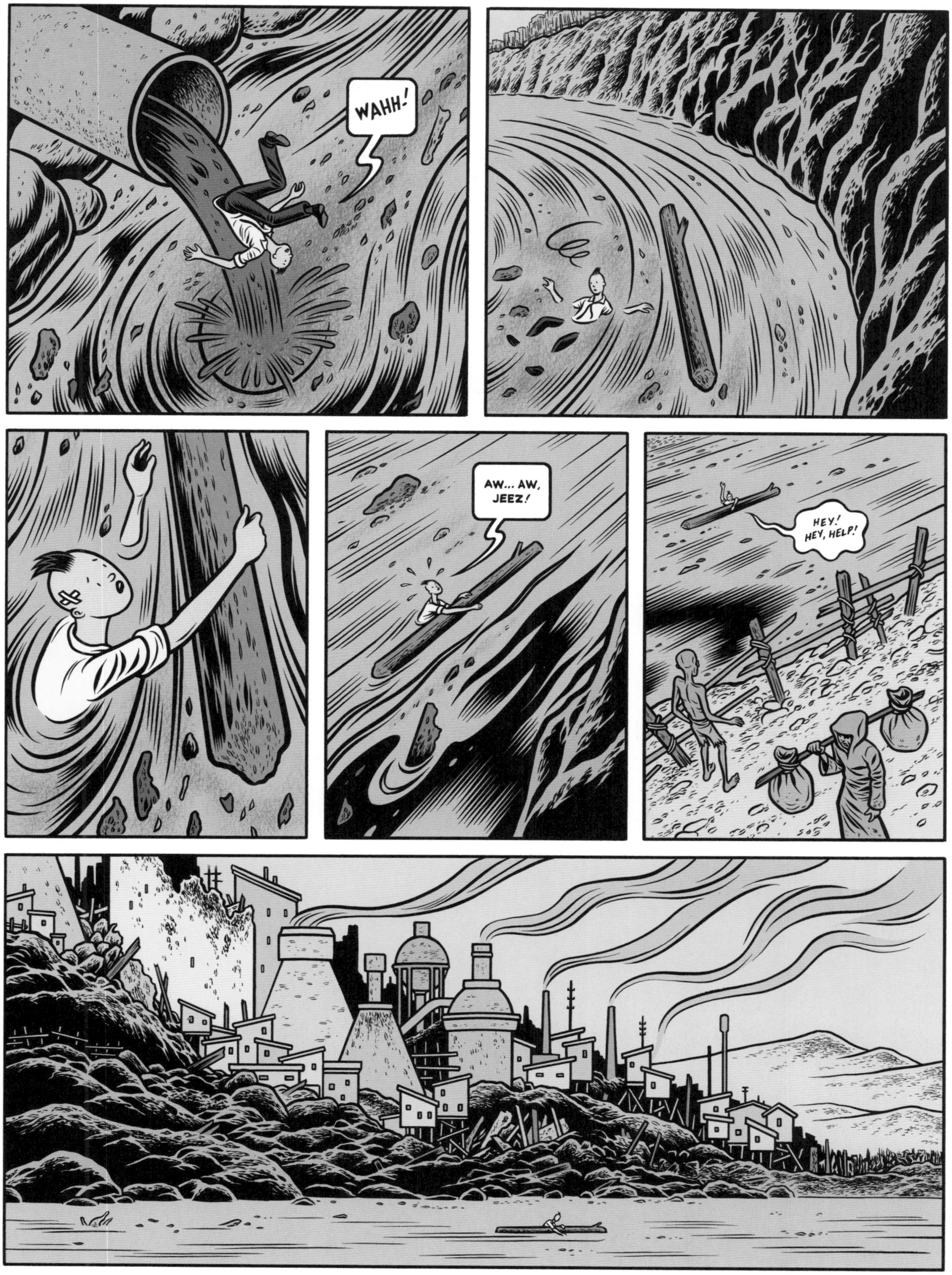
WAHH!
AW... AW, JEEZ!
HEY! HEY, HELP!

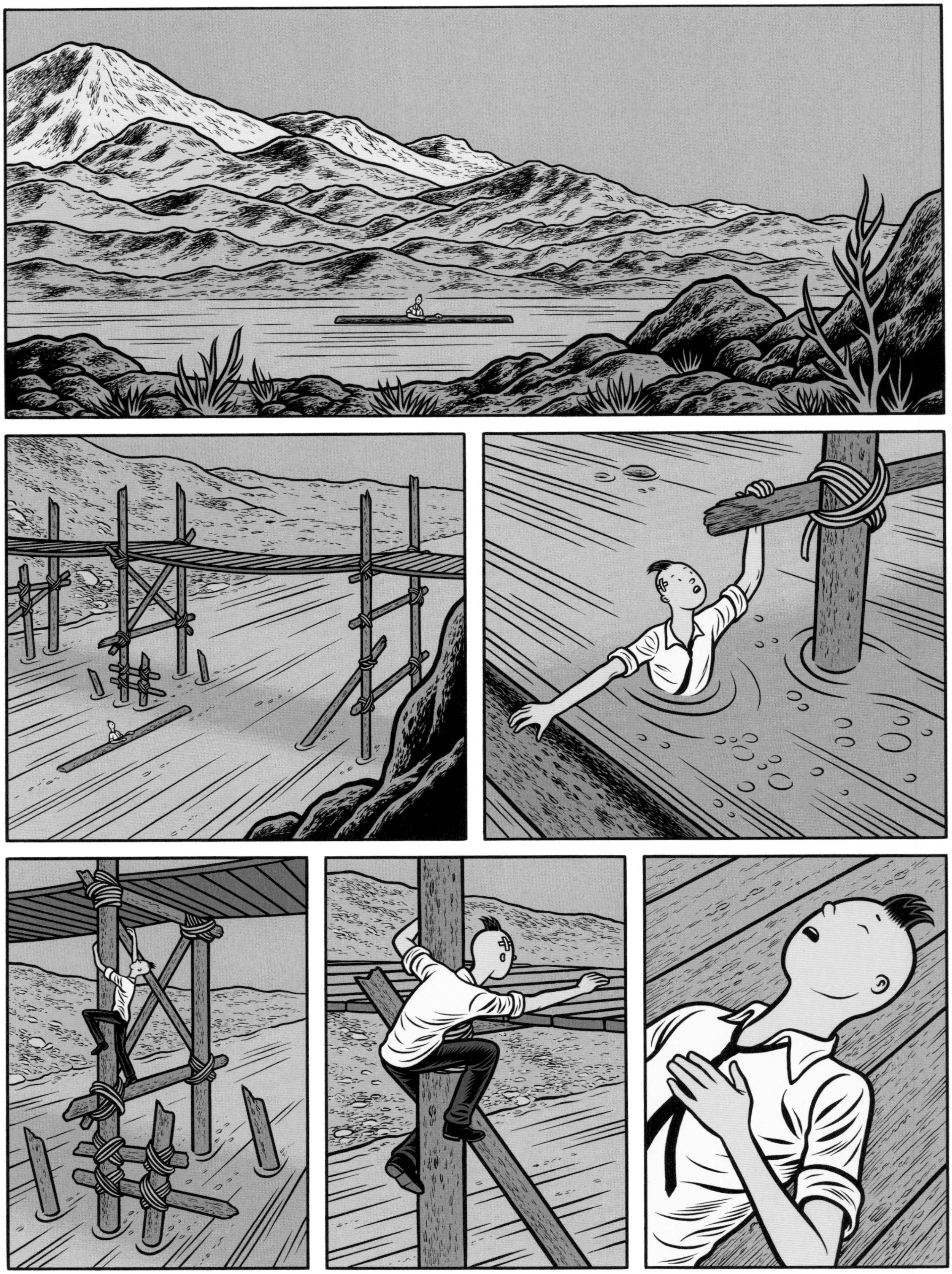

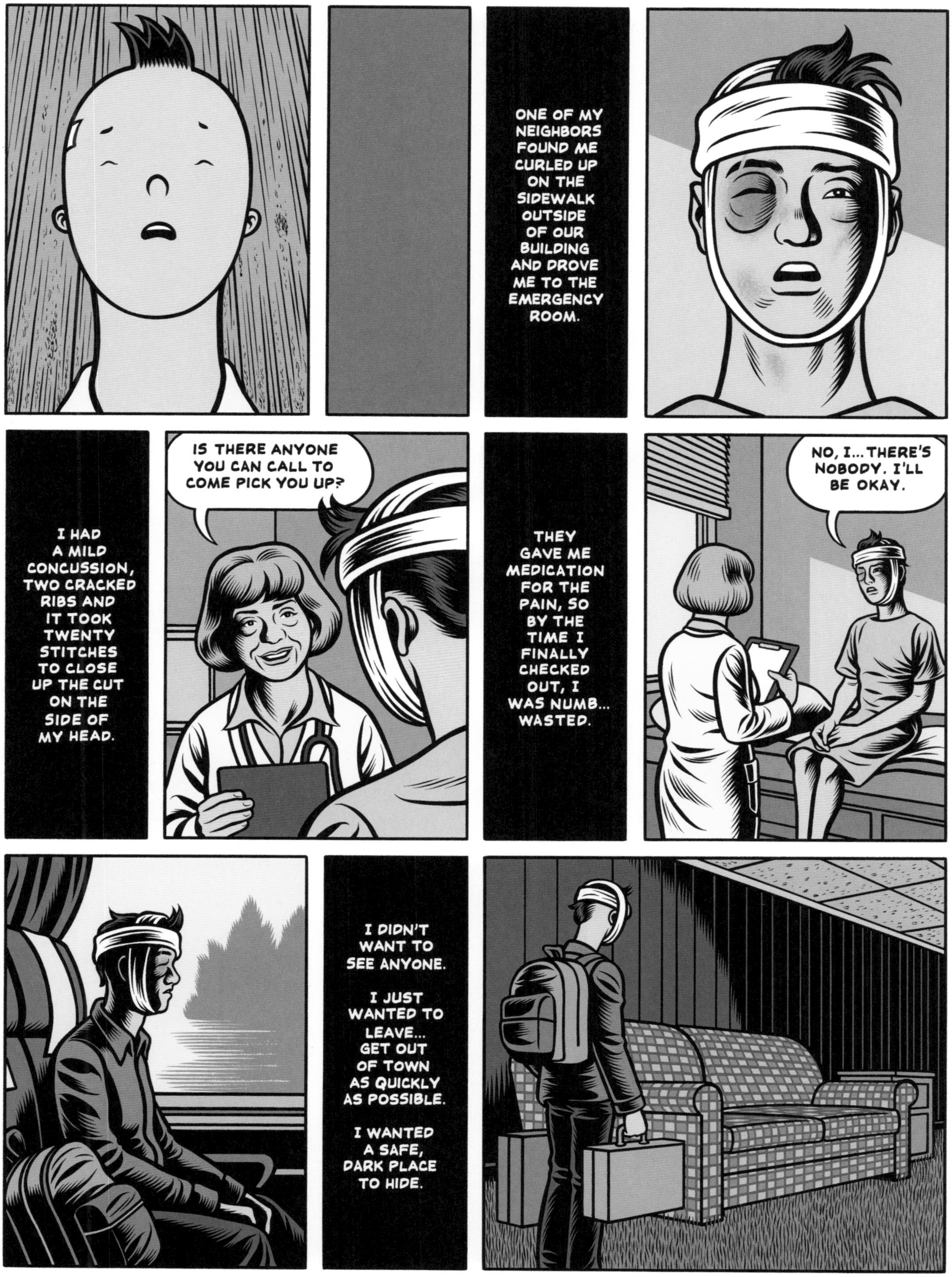

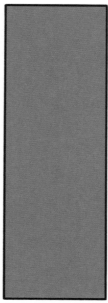

ONE OF MY NEIGHBORS FOUND ME CURLED UP ON THE SIDEWALK OUTSIDE OF OUR BUILDING AND DROVE ME TO THE EMERGENCY ROOM.
I HAD A MILD CONCUSSION, TWO CRACKED RIBS AND IT TOOK TWENTY STITCHES TO CLOSE UP THE CUT ON THE SIDE OF MY HEAD.
IS THERE ANYONE YOU CAN CALL TO COME PICK YOU UP?
THEY GAVE ME MEDICATION FOR THE PAIN, SO BY THE TIME I FINALLY CHECKED OUT, I WAS NUMB... WASTED.
NO, I... THERE'S NOBODY. I'LL BE OKAY.
I DIDN'T WANT TO SEE ANYONE.
I JUST WANTED TO LEAVE... GET OUT OF TOWN AS QUICKLY AS POSSIBLE.
I WANTED A SAFE, DARK PLACE TO HIDE.

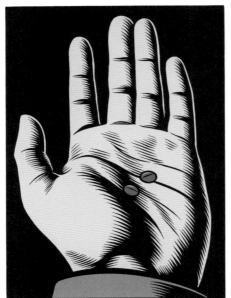

THE TELEVISION WAS ALWAYS ON. HE'D COMPLAIN ENDLESSLY ABOUT HOW STUPID ALL THE SHOWS WERE...

BUT HE'D WATCH THEM ANYWAY. ...COULDN'T BE BOTHERED TO GET UP AND CHANGE THE CHANNEL.

...THAT WAS MY JOB IF I HAPPENED TO BE AROUND.

SHOULD I TRY TEN? I THINK "HAPPY DAYS" IS ON.

AW, DON'T WORRY ABOUT THAT CRAP...COME OVER HERE AND LET ME SHOW YOU SOMETHING.

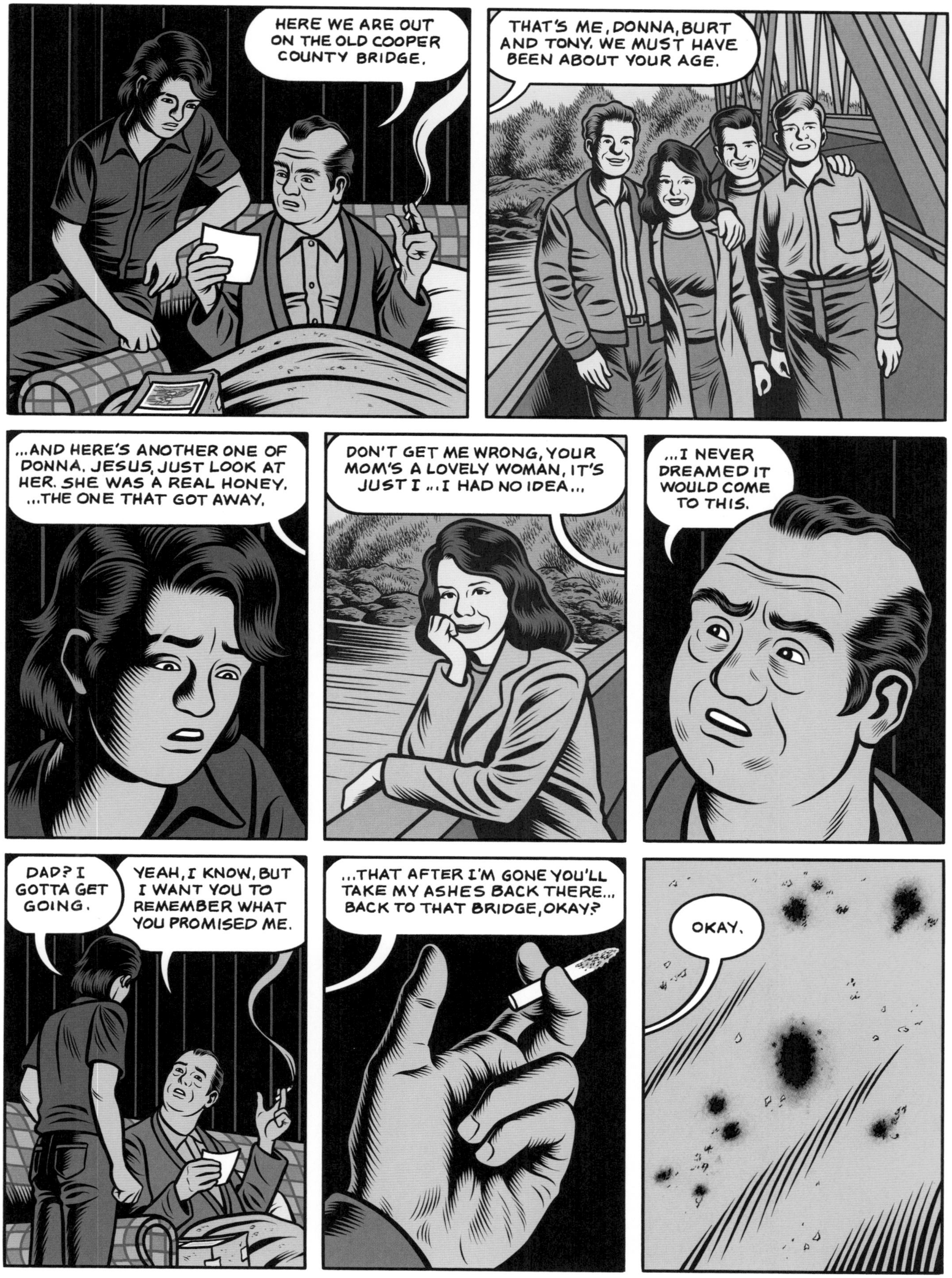
HERE WE ARE OUT ON THE OLD COOPER COUNTY BRIDGE.
THAT'S ME, DONNA, BURT AND TONY. WE MUST HAVE BEEN ABOUT YOUR AGE.
...AND HERE'S ANOTHER ONE OF DONNA. JESUS, JUST LOOK AT HER. SHE WAS A REAL HONEY. ...THE ONE THAT GOT AWAY.
DON'T GET ME WRONG, YOUR MOM'S A LOVELY WOMAN, IT'S JUST I ...I HAD NO IDEA...
...I NEVER DREAMED IT WOULD COME TO THIS.
DAD? I GOTTA GET GOING.
YEAH, I KNOW, BUT I WANT YOU TO REMEMBER WHAT YOU PROMISED ME.
...THAT AFTER I'M GONE YOU'LL TAKE MY ASHES BACK THERE... BACK TO THAT BRIDGE, OKAY?
OKAY.

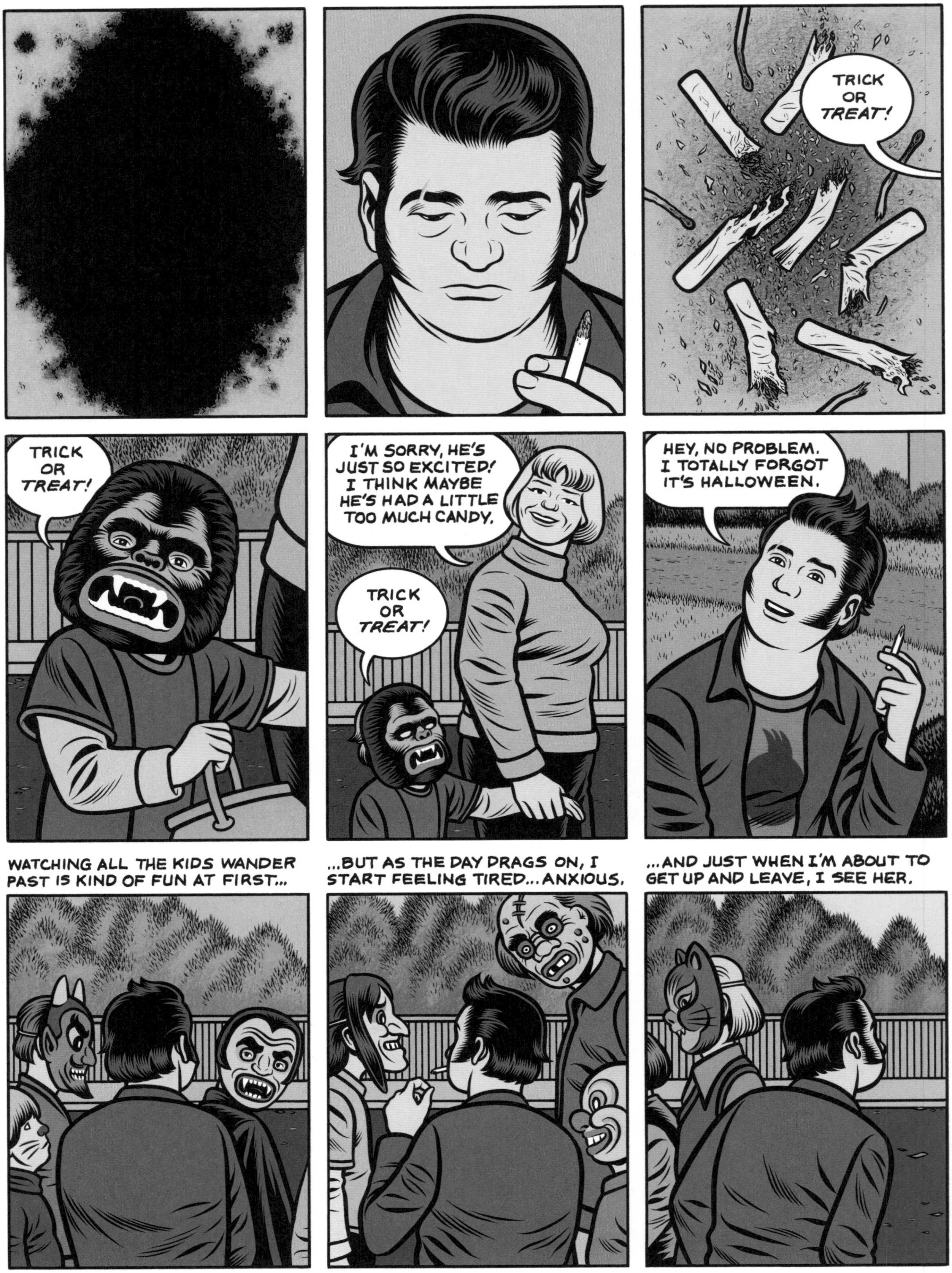
TRICK OR TREAT!
TRICK OR TREAT!
I'M SORRY, HE'S JUST SO EXCITED! I THINK MAYBE HE'S HAD A LITTLE TOO MUCH CANDY.
TRICK OR TREAT!
HEY, NO PROBLEM. I TOTALLY FORGOT IT'S HALLOWEEN.
WATCHING ALL THE KIDS WANDER PAST IS KIND OF FUN AT FIRST...
...BUT AS THE DAY DRAGS ON, I START FEELING TIRED... ANXIOUS.
...AND JUST WHEN I'M ABOUT TO GET UP AND LEAVE, I SEE HER.

HEY, SARAH...I HAPPENED TO BE IN THE CITY AND...AND THOUGHT I MIGHT LOOK YOU UP.

NICKY CALLED...TOLD ME SHE SAW YOU AT A CONCERT LAST WEEK.

DANNY? THIS IS DOUG. CAN YOU SAY HELLO?

HELLO.

WHY DON'T YOU TAKE YOUR MASK OFF SO DOUG CAN GET A BETTER LOOK AT YOU?

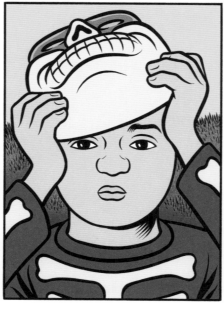

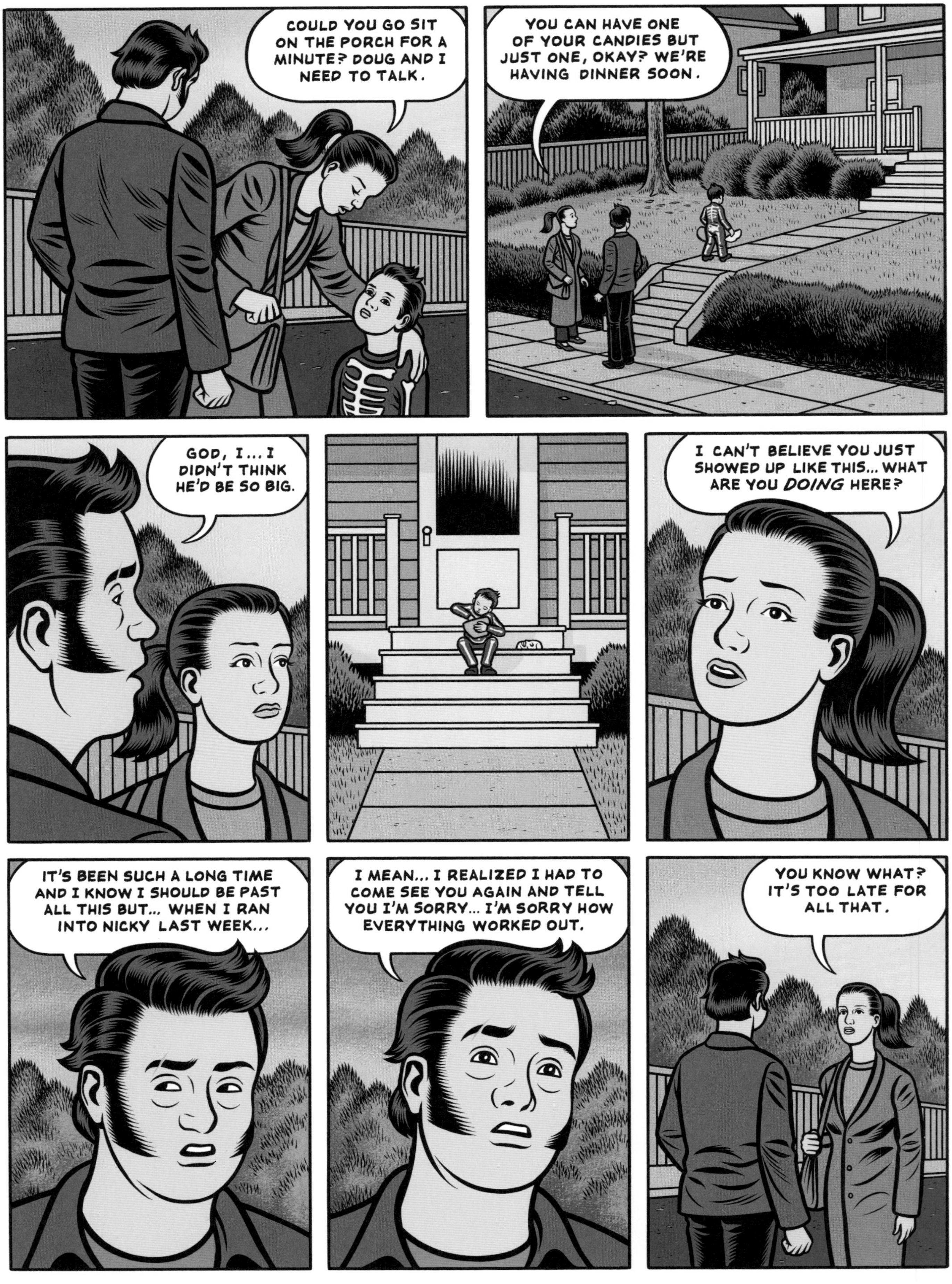
COULD YOU GO SIT ON THE PORCH FOR A MINUTE? DOUG AND I NEED TO TALK.
YOU CAN HAVE ONE OF YOUR CANDIES BUT JUST ONE, OKAY? WE'RE HAVING DINNER SOON.
GOD, I... I DIDN'T THINK HE'D BE SO BIG.
I CAN'T BELIEVE YOU JUST SHOWED UP LIKE THIS... WHAT ARE YOU *DOING* HERE?
IT'S BEEN SUCH A LONG TIME AND I KNOW I SHOULD BE PAST ALL THIS BUT... WHEN I RAN INTO NICKY LAST WEEK...
I MEAN... I REALIZED I HAD TO COME SEE YOU AGAIN AND TELL YOU I'M SORRY... I'M SORRY HOW EVERYTHING WORKED OUT.
YOU KNOW WHAT? IT'S TOO LATE FOR ALL THAT.

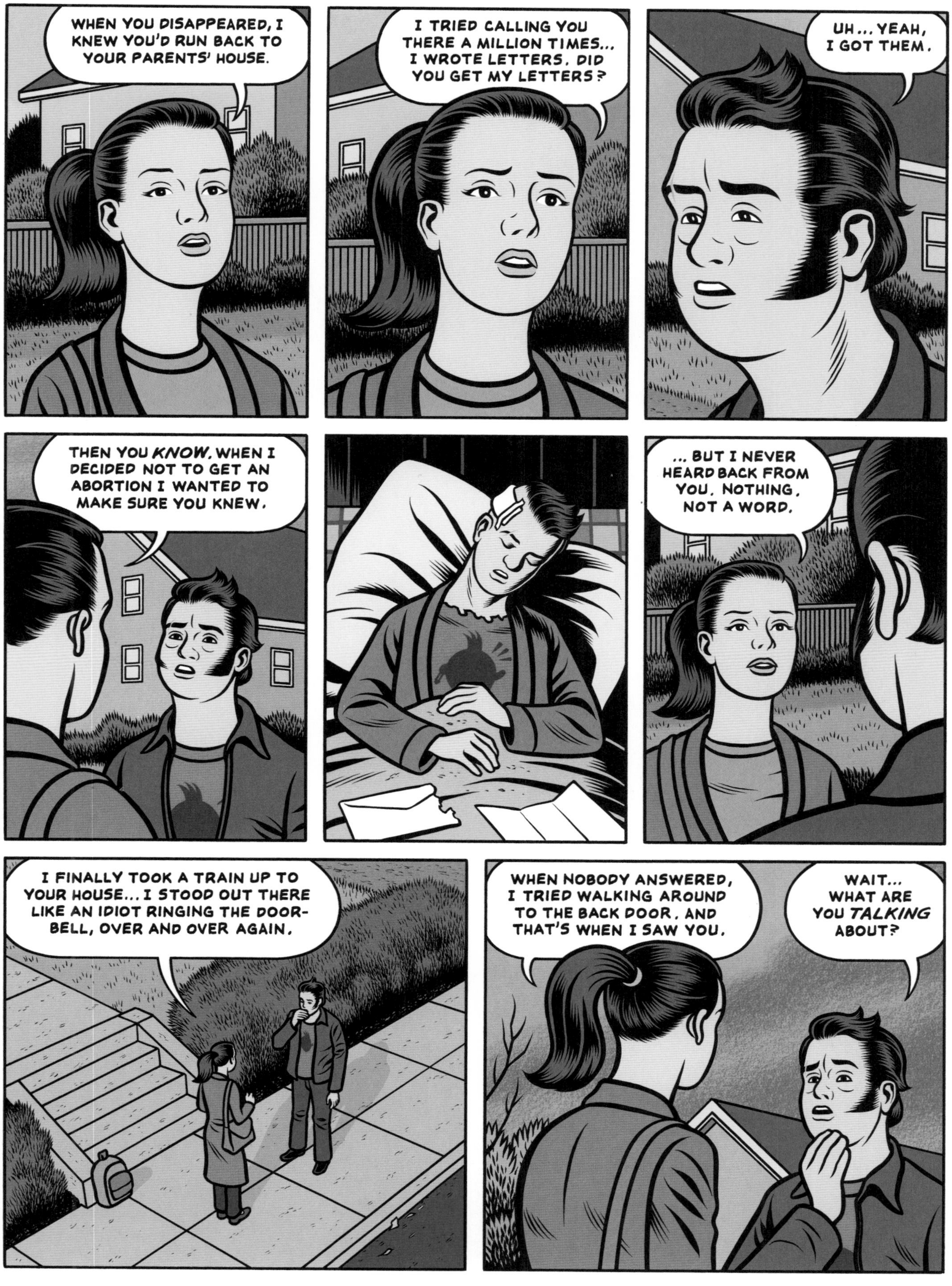
WHEN YOU DISAPPEARED, I KNEW YOU'D RUN BACK TO YOUR PARENTS' HOUSE.
I TRIED CALLING YOU THERE A MILLION TIMES... I WROTE LETTERS. DID YOU GET MY LETTERS?
UH... YEAH, I GOT THEM.
THEN YOU *KNOW*. WHEN I DECIDED NOT TO GET AN ABORTION I WANTED TO MAKE SURE YOU KNEW.
... BUT I NEVER HEARD BACK FROM YOU. NOTHING. NOT A WORD.
I FINALLY TOOK A TRAIN UP TO YOUR HOUSE... I STOOD OUT THERE LIKE AN IDIOT RINGING THE DOOR-BELL, OVER AND OVER AGAIN.
WHEN NOBODY ANSWERED, I TRIED WALKING AROUND TO THE BACK DOOR, AND THAT'S WHEN I SAW YOU.
WAIT... WHAT ARE YOU *TALKING* ABOUT?

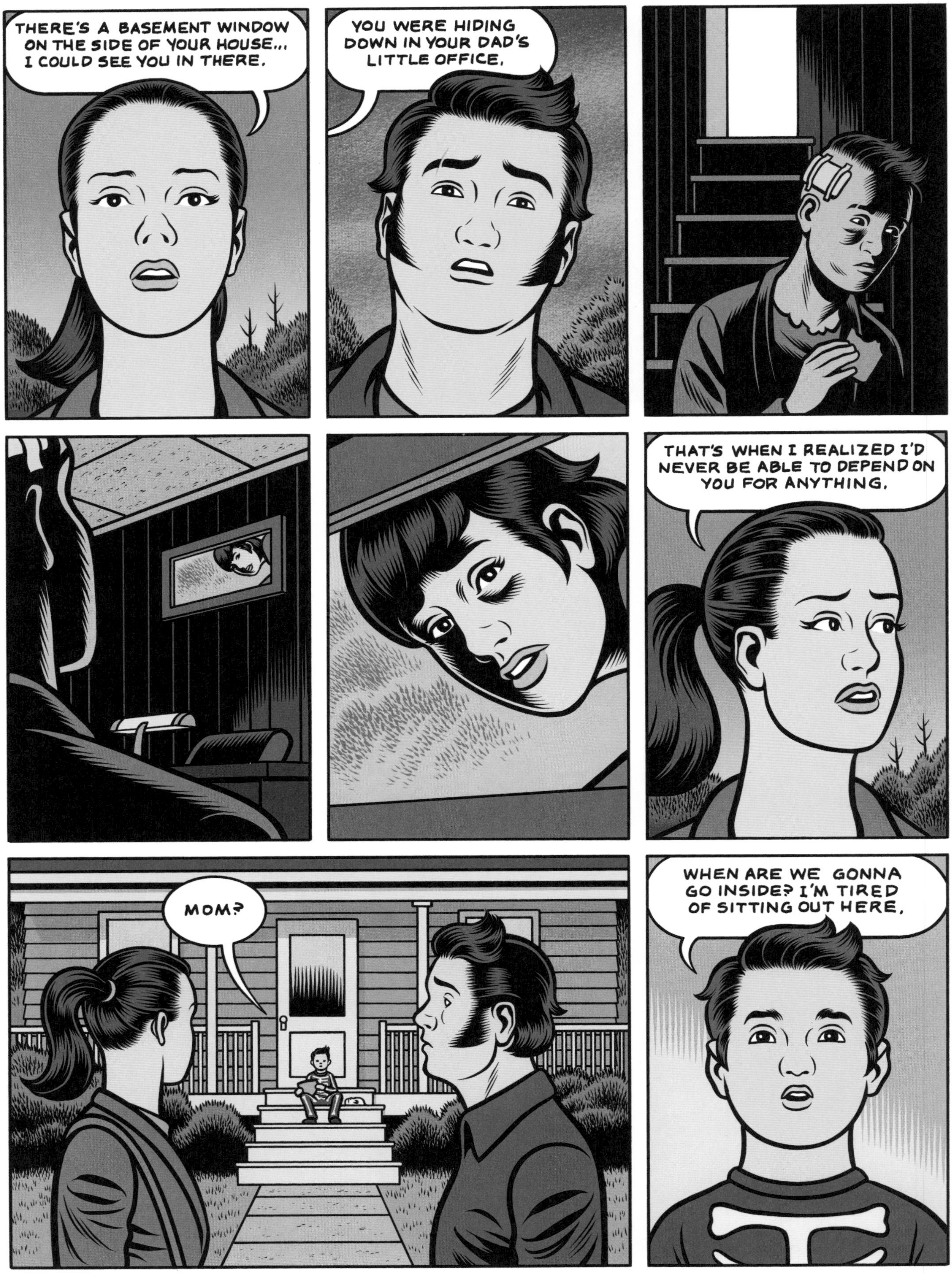
THERE'S A BASEMENT WINDOW ON THE SIDE OF YOUR HOUSE... I COULD SEE YOU IN THERE.
YOU WERE HIDING DOWN IN YOUR DAD'S LITTLE OFFICE.
THAT'S WHEN I REALIZED I'D NEVER BE ABLE TO DEPEND ON YOU FOR ANYTHING.
MOM?
WHEN ARE WE GONNA GO INSIDE? I'M TIRED OF SITTING OUT HERE.

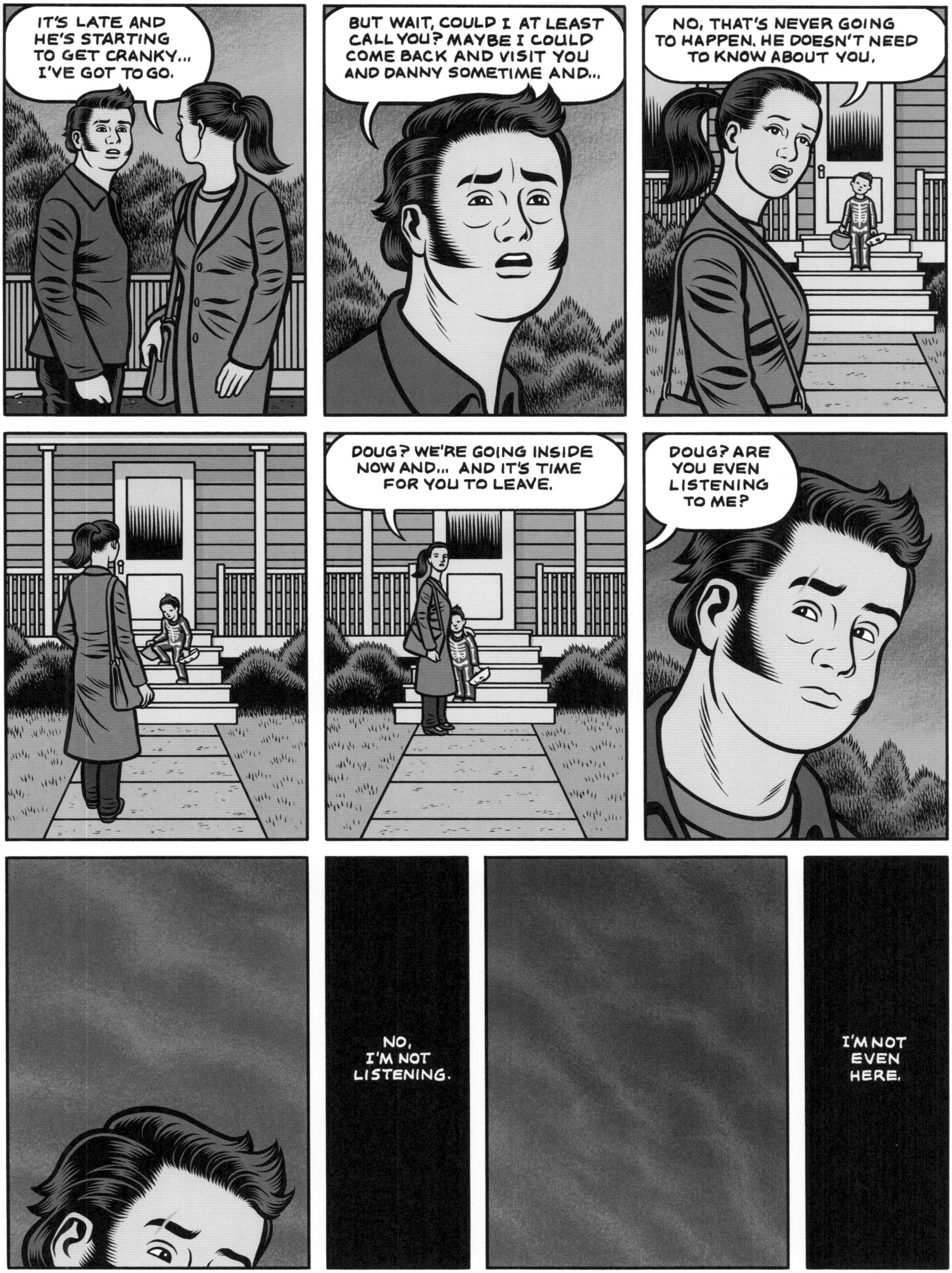
IT'S LATE AND HE'S STARTING TO GET CRANKY... I'VE GOT TO GO.
BUT WAIT, COULD I AT LEAST CALL YOU? MAYBE I COULD COME BACK AND VISIT YOU AND DANNY SOMETIME AND...
NO, THAT'S NEVER GOING TO HAPPEN. HE DOESN'T NEED TO KNOW ABOUT YOU.
DOUG? WE'RE GOING INSIDE NOW AND... AND IT'S TIME FOR YOU TO LEAVE.
DOUG? ARE YOU EVEN LISTENING TO ME?
NO, I'M NOT LISTENING.
I'M NOT EVEN HERE.

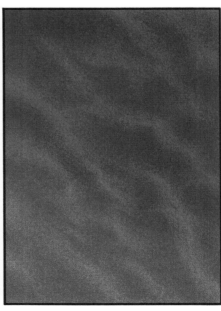

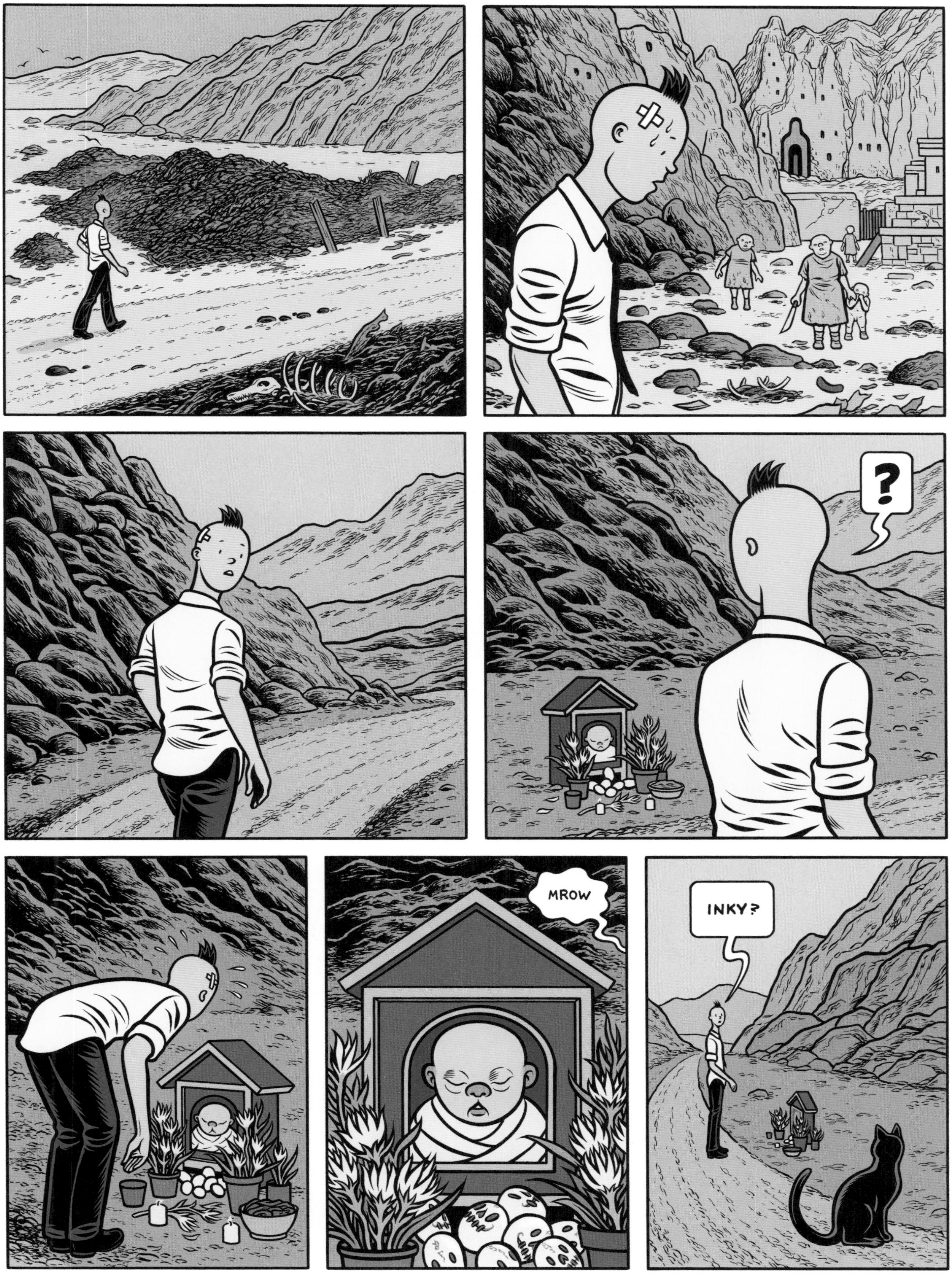
?
MROW
INKY?

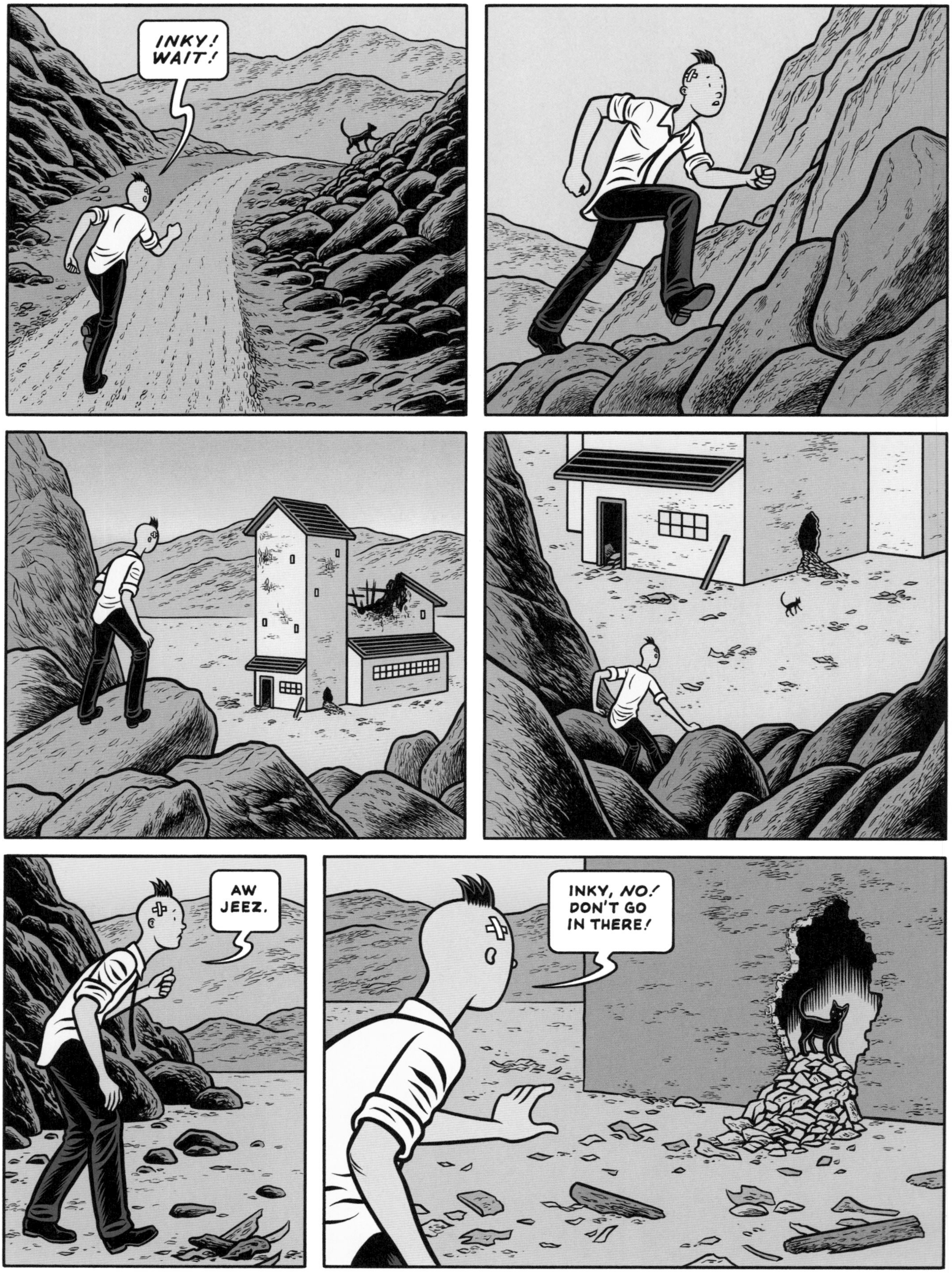
INKY! WAIT!
AW JEEZ.
INKY, NO! DON'T GO IN THERE!

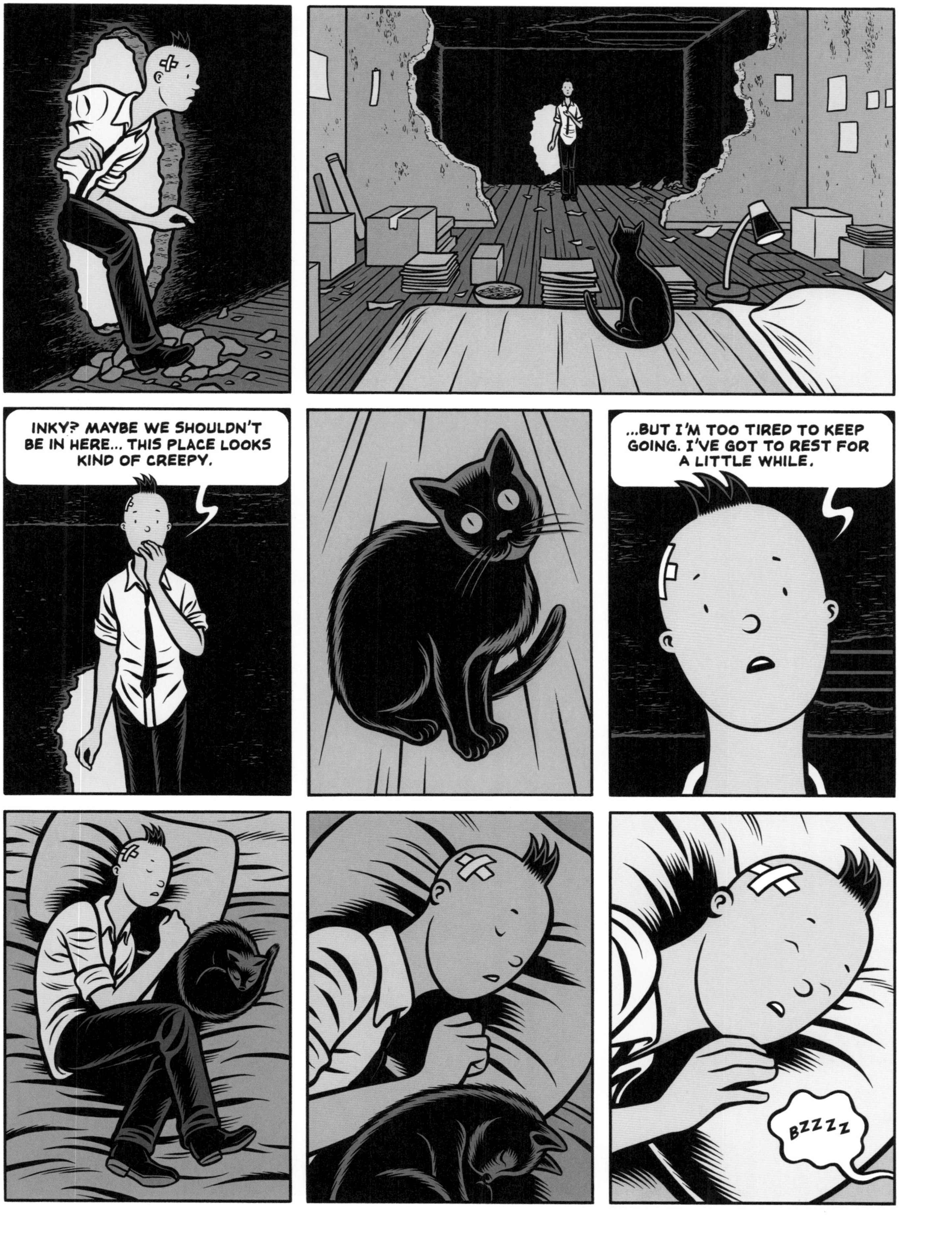
INKY? MAYBE WE SHOULDN'T BE IN HERE... THIS PLACE LOOKS KIND OF CREEPY.
...BUT I'M TOO TIRED TO KEEP GOING. I'VE GOT TO REST FOR A LITTLE WHILE.
BZZZZ

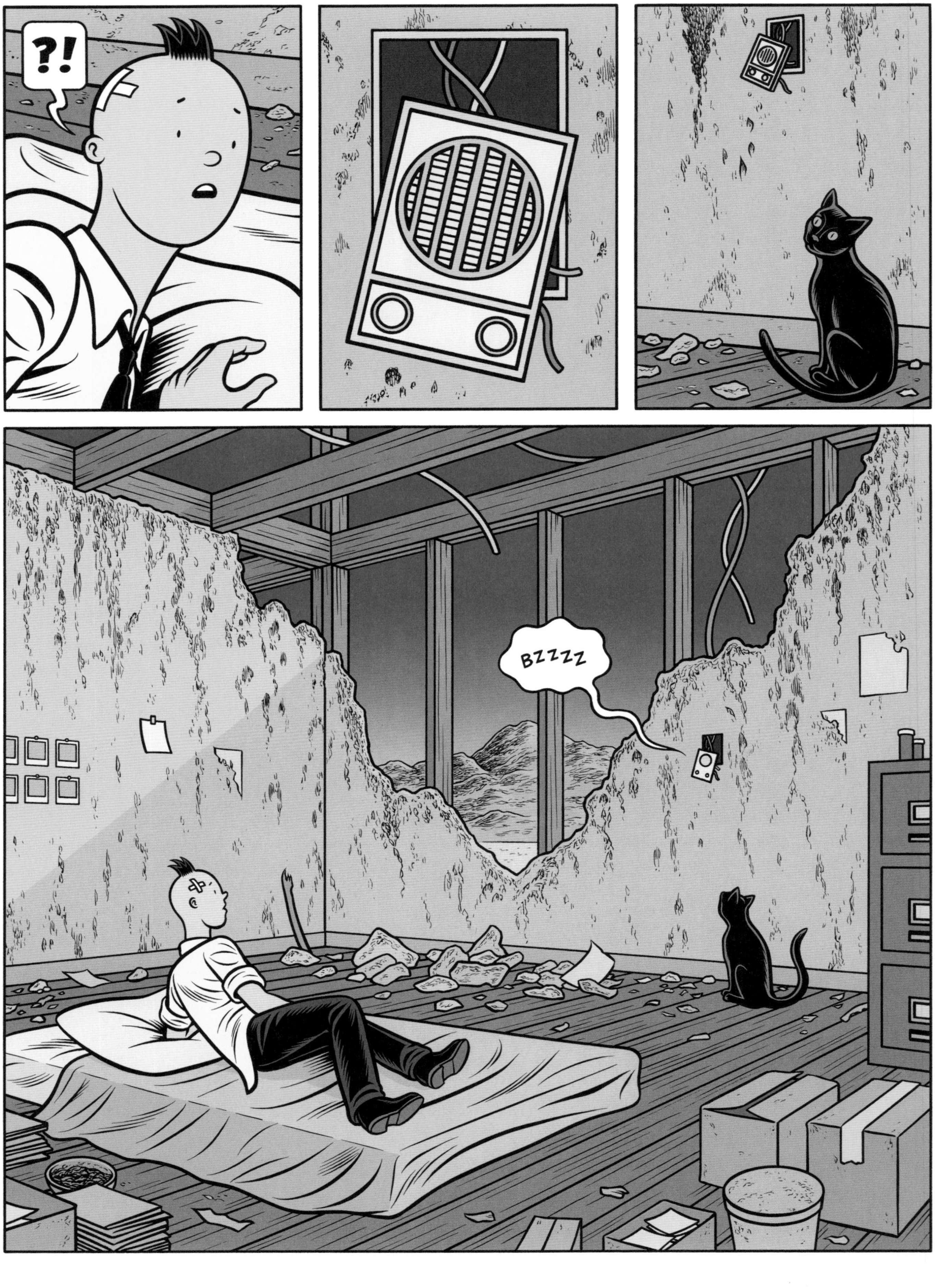
?!
BZZZZ

THE END

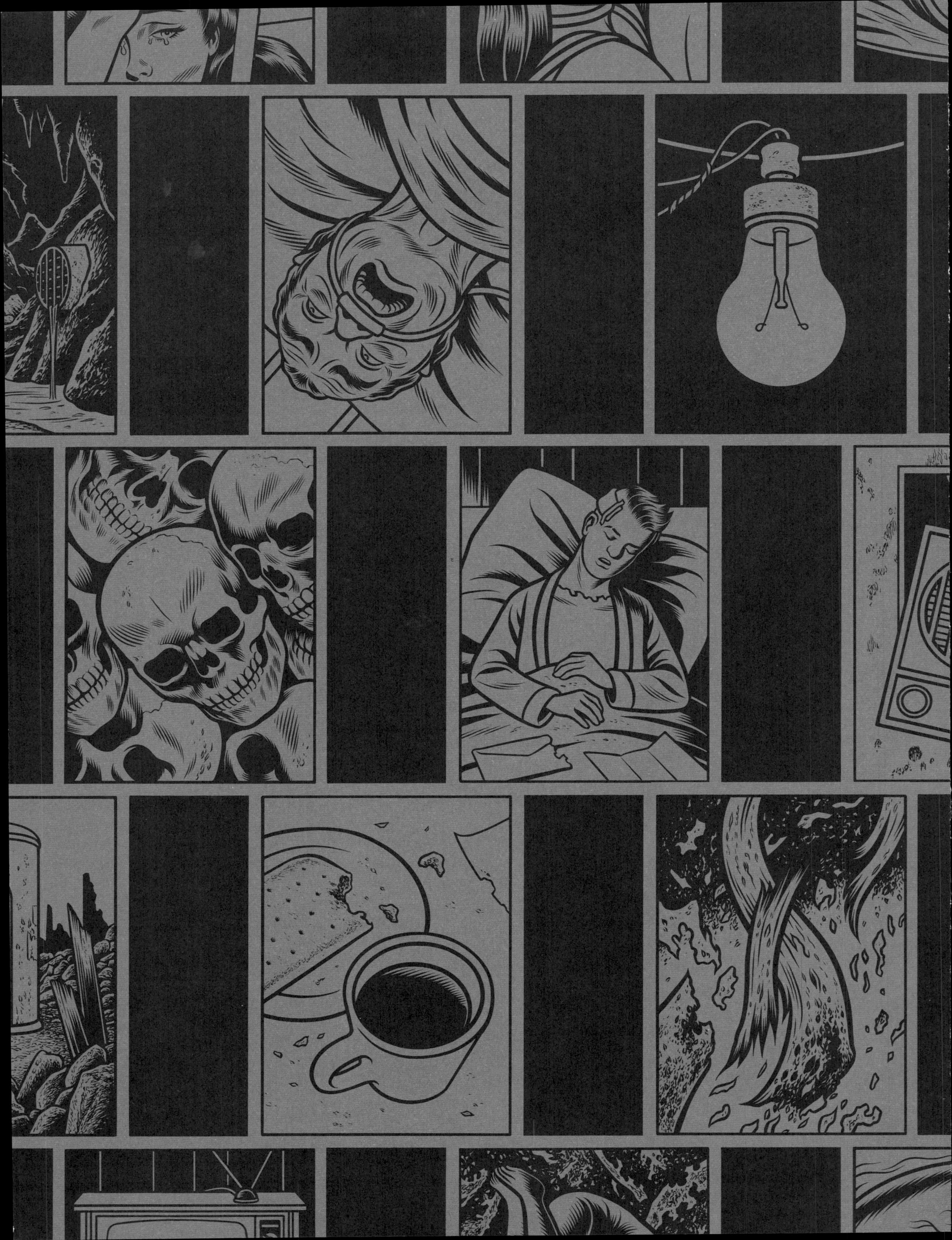